JKtW

SALAMAINE'S CURSE

THE MAPMAKER'S SONS 2

SALAMAINE'S CURSE

THE MAPMAKER'S SONS 2

by
V. L. BURGESS

illustrated by
JON BERKELEY

MOVE BOOKS

Note from the Publisher:
*The Move Books team is committed to inspiring boys to read. We want to change
the way boys look at reading. Thank you for your support.*

Text copyright © 2013 by V. L. Burgess
Illustration copyright © by Jon Berkeley
Book Design by Virginia Pope
Back cover parchment background © iStockphoto.com/tomograf

All rights reserved. Published by Move Books LLC.

Library of Congress Control Number: 2013941511

10 9 8 7 6 5 4 3 2 1   11 12 13 14 15 16
Printed and bound in the U.S.A.
First edition, October 2013

P.O. Box 183
Beacon Falls, Connecticut, 06403

For BOB, DAVID, and CATHERINE
— *V.L. Burgess*

for RUBEN and ALAN
— *Jon Berkeley*

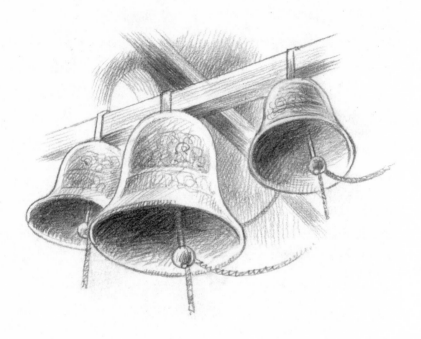

CHAPTER ONE

THE
FORBIDDEN LAKE

Thomas Hawkins stood at the edge of the Forbidden Lake. It had another name, of course, an official name, but nobody ever used it. Tom couldn't even remember what it was. He only knew that at the Lost Preparatory Academy for Boys, anything that might lead to the students actually enjoying themselves was, naturally, forbidden.

Especially the lake.

And definitely, *definitely*, the lake at midnight.

But it was spring. The ice and snow that had covered the academy grounds for endless months had finally melted, giving way to soft, grassy fields. Shimmering rays of sunshine warmed the air. Or at least the grass looked soft and the air seemed warm. Hard to tell when he spent most of his waking hours locked away in a classroom.

Which was exactly what had brought Tom to the lake. It wasn't that he deliberately tried to disobey the rules. But Headmaster Lost's rigid schedules, endless exams, and not to mention the constant clamor of bells wore on his nerves. On *everybody's* nerves. All he wanted to do was loosen things up a bit. Have a little fun.

Kidnapping Fred and sending him on a solo midnight sail

1

across the lake seemed like the perfect antidote to the dull drudgery of their days. It was, after all, spring.

Excited whispers and rustling branches echoed through the woods. Tom glanced over his shoulder at the guys behind him and grinned.

"How's he doing?"

"I think he's scared," a voice called back.

"No, he's not!" someone else shouted. "He's having fun! Aren't you, Fred?"

Fred wobbled in response as the gardening cart to which he was strapped hit a deep rut in the trail. He teetered precariously to the right, then swayed left as the boys pushing the cart overcorrected their mistake.

"Don't drop him! You'll crack his head open."

"Relax. He's fine." They shoved the cart out of the rut and bounded down the trail.

Fred was the newest addition to the Lost Academy family. He came to them as a result of a private donation made to the school. The funds were supposed to be used for the students' enjoyment.

But Lost, brimming with satisfaction, had unveiled the life-sized statue—to whom the name Fred had somehow stuck—at an assembly earlier that week. The thrill of the gift had been underwhelming. The model of a perfect student, Fred had been sculpted with Latin and Greek textbooks tucked under his arm and a beaming smile on his face, as though he couldn't wait to get back to his room and spend his evening memorizing ancient irregular verbs.

Hunger for Knowledge, the plaque beneath him read. Looking at Fred, Tom thought *Hunger for Cupcakes, Chili Dogs, and Cheese Fries* would have been far more appropriate.

For not only did Fred arrive wearing the detested summer

uniform (short-sleeved shirt with tie, Bermuda shorts and knee socks, a beanie on his head), he had a little weight problem. His face was round, his cheeks plump, and he had a double chin. In what was probably a clumsy attempt to make Fred look younger, the sculptor had given him pudgy arms and thighs, dimpled hands, and a butt that swelled outward in embarrassing proportions, sort of like a certain type of monkey at the zoo.

When they heard about the donation, Tom and his friends had spent weeks convincing themselves Lost would finally give in and buy them Xboxes for the common rooms.

Instead they got Fred.

Tom's eyes narrowed in on the beanie. A pirate's hat and a few other things would definitely make Fred more interesting . . . and Lost more furious.

His friends reached the beach. Or rather, what passed for a beach—a broad expanse of packed dirt that stretched half the length of a football field, then sloped gently downward until it dipped into the edge of the water. The lake was quiet. Nothing but shimmering moonlight reflected on the surface, coupled with the gentle lapping of water against the shore.

Their plan was simple. Two boats tied together with rope, one for Tom, one for Fred. Tom would row the lead boat to the center of the lake and cut Fred loose. All he had to do after that was row back to the beach and rejoin his friends, leaving Fred adrift. The look on Lost's face when he discovered his beloved Fred had turned pirate and taken a midnight sail . . . now *that* was something he couldn't wait to see.

The group split up. Two guys ran to the boathouse to borrow a couple of old wooden rowboats (proof that at some point in its history students of the academy had been allowed to enjoy the lake, despite Lost declaring it Officially Off Limits).

The remaining boys untied Fred. Fortunately for them

he wasn't as heavy as he looked. Fred was as hollow as a cheap chocolate Easter bunny. They managed to lower him to the ground without shattering him into pieces or splitting off an arm.

Now the only thing left to do was to prepare Fred for launch. It didn't take much, just a few items borrowed from the theater department. A skull-and-crossbones hat slapped over his beanie, a toy parrot stuck on his shoulder, a rusty old cutlass duct taped to his wrist, and the transformation from chubby student to chubby pirate was complete.

"You sure this is a good idea?" asked Matt Copley, Tom's best friend. Matt was both more cautious and smarter than Tom—or maybe being smarter made him more cautious. In any case, he looked worried.

Tom studied Fred, all decked out in his pirate finery, and smiled. "Absolutely."

"What if he sinks the boat?"

Good point.

"He won't."

They tested him out in the shallows, just in case, and got lucky. Fred's pose—his feet spread wide apart as though caught in mid-stride, just so *eager* to rush back and study—absorbed his weight and gave him greater stability. The boat rocked, but settled nicely in the water.

"Look, he's smiling! He likes it."

"Yeah, he's a natural," Tom deadpanned.

Matt gave a shaky smile. "Lost'll kill you if he finds out you were behind this. You're already on his list."

True.

But as Matt pointed out, Tom had already made Lost's infamous demerit list. Looking at it that way, he had very little to lose. Besides, hadn't Lost himself said the funds were to be used for the students' enjoyment? At least this they would enjoy.

A couple of guys held Fred's boat steady, while a few more held Tom's boat as he climbed aboard to keep it from rocking. He grabbed the oars and glanced at the distance he needed to cover. Ten minutes max and he'd be back ashore. Ten minutes after that and they'd all be in their dorm rooms, sound asleep, with nothing to do but wait for the morning bell.

He settled himself with his back to the lake and slipped the oars into the water. But the moment the oars broke the surface something caught his ear.

"Quiet!" he hissed, motioning for his friends to keep their voices down. He tilted his head toward the water. "Did you hear that?"

"Yeah," replied one of the guys on shore. "It's the wind."

Tom shot a glance at the surrounding woods. Sure enough, the wind was picking up. A steady breeze rustled through the leaves. But what he'd heard hadn't come from the direction of the trees. It sounded as though it had come from deep within the water itself. He glanced over his shoulder at the lake. Studied its picture-perfect, mirror-like surface.

Matt frowned. "You all right, Tom?"

"Yeah. I'm fine."

He hesitated, then tested the water with his hand. Freezing cold. So cold it stung. But that wasn't the worst of it. The moment the oar dipped beneath the surface of the water, the lake seemed to shimmer with menace, rolling and rippling like waves in a funhouse mirror.

He scanned the lake but could find nothing wrong. Whatever had spooked him was gone. Probably just a trick of the moonlight, he decided. He flexed his fingers and clenched his fist to bring warmth back to his hand.

"You sure you don't want me to come with you?" Matt pressed.

Tom considered the offer. Actually, who he wanted with him was his brother, Porter. Ridiculous. Tom knew that better than anybody. In the first place, he hadn't heard from Porter in months. Secondly, even if Porter was there, most likely he'd just tell Tom he was acting like an idiot, that the entire stunt was juvenile, and that he had better things to do with his time.

Tom shook his head. "Nah, I got it. I'll be right back."

Another breeze, stronger this time, blew across the lake. Dark clouds raced across the moon. The air felt heavy, tinged with an electric charge. A storm was heading their way. It hadn't been there a minute ago, but there was no mistaking that the weather was turning. Tom's excitement faded, replaced by a sudden urgency to dump Fred as quickly as possible and get back to his dorm.

His friends gave the boats a gentle shove, and he and Fred cast off. Tom took up the oars and rowed toward the center of the lake, careful to keep his strokes slow and steady so as not to topple Fred. Shouts and laughter echoed around him, filling the night air. Getting back into the spirit of the adventure, Tom smiled and relaxed a bit, easing his way forward.

The wind steadily picked up. It was stronger now, strong enough to ripple the water and blow hundreds of miniature white-capped waves across the surface of the lake. Tom dug the oars in, only to discover he didn't need them. Rowing was no longer necessary. The moment he left the shallows he was caught in a current that rushed them toward the center of the lake.

They were moving fast, much faster than his strokes could have possibly carried them. He glanced at Fred, who bobbed along behind him with his fake grin plastered on his fake face, the breeze ruffling the feathers on his toy parrot, looking as though he was having the time of his life.

Alarm surged through Tom. He had heard of riptides in the ocean, but was it possible for there to be riptides in a lake? He didn't know. He fought against the current, dragging the oars in the water to create resistance, but the force carrying them was too strong to break.

The current stopped, depositing them in the icy heart of the lake. Tom's boat gently rocked, the water softly lapping against the hull. Eerie stillness settled over him. A thick cloud hung across the moon. Like a velvet curtain shut, all light was gone. He peered into the darkness but couldn't make out anything.

Then he heard it. The sound he'd heard before he'd left shore. The sound he'd allowed himself to believe was only the wind rustling through the trees. This time there was no mistaking it. There was no pretending it was anything other than what it was: a low, menacing growl that ended in a long, drawn-out hiss. The hair on the back of his neck stood up as the noise cut through the night air.

Forks of lightening flashed in the distance as a peal of thunder cracked overhead.

Tom felt his thoughts, senses, and intuition finally click in the proper order. Horrified understanding swept through him. A violent storm was blowing in. The door between worlds was opening—which meant the evil that existed in Porter's world could come through to his.

Had come through to his.

A gust of wind parted the clouds, allowing him a glimmer of moonlight to shine across the surface of the lake. His sight abruptly returned. Tom looked down.

His gaze locked on a shadow lurking just beneath the surface of the water. A pair of menacing red eyes peered up at him.

Tom's heart slammed against the wall of his chest, then began beating at triple its normal rate. He tore his eyes away from the creature's scorching gaze long enough to size up the rest of the thing.

Some sort of serpent, he guessed. Long and thick, it slithered through the water, curling around the edges of his boat like an enormous snake. The serpent's mottled skin—black and gray and pea green—rippled as it moved, evidence of the bulky muscles that propelled it. There was no sleek beauty about it. No fairy-tale suggestion of a poor lost creature searching for its way home. This was a monster, pure and simple.

A monster that was now glaring at him . . . hungrily.

CHAPTER TWO

FOLLY STRIKES

Frozen in horror, Tom watched as the serpent slowly heaved its upper torso from the water. Assuming a cobra-like position, it swayed back and forth, its radar-like focus locked on him. In that instant, Tom's world narrowed. His entire attention shrank to two basic elements: the serpent and the lake. His rowboat, which until that moment he'd considered sturdy and solid, now seemed a puny, insignificant defense.

He needed a weapon. Fast.

He cast a panicked glance around the boat's interior. Nothing. Nothing but the wooden oars balanced on his lap. Nothing but Fred drifting along behind him, decked out in a ridiculous pirate hat, with a toy parrot riding on his shoulder and a metal cutlass duct-taped to his wrist.

The cutlass. It was old and it was rusty, but it was a sword. If he could just get to Fred's boat without losing his balance and tipping himself overboard . . .

His gaze locked on the serpent, Tom carefully rose to his feet. His boat rocked. Fred swayed. Tom looked at the sword. The serpent, as though guessing his intent, let out a long, angry hiss.

The water surrounding the creature began to froth and foam. The serpent twisted its body into a compact coil, collapsing in on itself, gathering energy like a tightly wound spring. It snapped the tip of its tail into the air and shook it, producing a sharp, vibrating clatter similar to a rattlesnake's.

That was the only warning Tom had.

The serpent shot toward him at torpedo-like speed. But instead of ramming his boat, the serpent performed an abrupt ninety degree turn and slithered along the side of it, rubbing its body along the wooden length as though scratching an itch. Tom's hull tilted wildly, nearly tossing him overboard. He caught his balance and watched as the serpent slithered in a sinister figure eight, twisting itself between his boat and Fred's, as though daring Tom to make the leap.

The boats rocked and pitched, knocked about by the creature's enormous weight and length. As the serpent reached the bow of Tom's boat, it abruptly swerved from its menacing orbit. Moving with astonishing agility given its size, its head and neck shot out of the water. It stopped just short of Tom's face, its burning red eyes inches away, its fangs glistening, its slimy forked tongue almost tickling his nose.

The creature released a shrill hiss. A gust of blazing hot, foul breath brushed Tom's skin, fanning his face like a blast of air from a roaring fire.

Tom let out a frantic yelp and lurched backward. His sneakers slipped on the boat's wet floor. He lost his footing and fell hard, slamming his back against the boat's edge. White-hot shards of pain shot up his spine. He let out a low groan and rolled onto his hands and knees in time to see the serpent, wearing an expression that could only be described as a sinister smirk, slide back into the murky depths. It was toying with him, Tom realized, playing some kind of twisted game. Anger surged through him, temporarily replacing the terror that had paralyzed him in place. Getting to his feet, he tightened his grip on an oar, brought it over his head, and swung it down hard. He hit the serpent's flesh, landing with a soft *splat* that did nothing to injure the creature or drive it away.

Instead, the creature's blood-red eyes flashed with fury.

Retaliation was swift and brutal. The serpent's tail shot out of the water and slammed against the boat. Wood splintered and cracked, flying everywhere, leaving a hole in the side of the boat the size of an enormous shark bite. Icy water poured in, drenching Tom's feet and ankles.

It was only a matter of minutes—maybe seconds—until his boat would sink. Left with no other option, Tom sprang into Fred's boat. The vessel rocked heavily toward the bow. He shifted to the stern, but the boat still wouldn't stabilize. It took him a second to realize why. Their boats remained securely tied together. As the lead boat continued to take on water, it was pulling Fred's boat down with it.

Tom lunged for the rope and fumbled with the knot, frantically tugging until it slipped loose. He set his boat free and watched it flounder, then sink beneath the murky water with an audible *glub, glub, glub*.

The serpent thrashed about in a state of frenzied excitement, as though searching for Tom in the boat's watery remains.

The cutlass. Now was his chance. Tom spun toward Fred and tugged at the duct tape that fixed the sword to his palm. He'd nearly worked it free when the sound of the serpent's rattle rang in his ear. Tom froze. His gaze shot to the lake. The creature's glowing red eyes watched him. Then, before he could react, it lifted its tail from the water and drew the hard, rattle-like tip down his cheek in a slow caress. Tom's blood went cold.

The serpent lunged. Tom, gripping the cutlass, twisted sideways and dove for the bottom of the boat. Having missed Tom, the serpent coiled its enormous tail around Fred, lifted the statue, and slammed it into the dark, frigid depths of the lake.

Seconds passed.

The creature coughed up a spray of feathers and whacked its tail against the water, leaving Tom with the distinct impression that it was *his head* the monster had hoped to devour, not Fred's toy parrot. And it was definitely not pleased with the substitution.

The serpent shot out of the water and lunged again. Its fiery eyes blazed, its fangs glistened. Tom ducked and swung his cutlass, aiming for the creature's throat.

He missed.

Instead of hitting the serpent's neck, his rusty blade sliced through the creature's tail, severing the rattle tip from the rest of its body. The serpent gave a shrill, high-pitched whine and arched out of the water, thrashing madly. Then gravity took hold of it. The full weight of its body collapsed on top of the boat, smashing it into a thousand pieces and pitching Tom into the lake.

Cold. Icy cold. The shock of it stabbed his skin like thousands of sharp, stinging needles driven into his body at once. His muscles locked in a spasm of protest, but fortunately he didn't need to swim. His life vest returned him to the surface. Gasping, Tom drew in a lungful of air. He brought up the cutlass and peered into the darkness, readying himself for the serpent's next attack.

But the water was eerily quiet. The creature was gone— at least for the moment. The only sign that the serpent had been there at all was the rattle tip of its amputated tail, which glowed a deep pinkish-orange as it bobbed in the water in front of him. Tom stared at it, totally transfixed. The rattle was unlike anything he'd ever seen before. It looked like some rare jewel that had come to life before his very eyes. Unable to stop himself, he reached for it.

A splash sounded behind him. Tom whirled around, his heart beating wildly.

Fred. The statue popped to the surface. Apparently his hollow build gave him enough buoyancy to float. Fred stared at the sky with an expression of mild surprise on his face, as though he hadn't expected to find himself in a lake at midnight, victim of a sea serpent attack.

Tom knew exactly how he felt.

Icy cold seeped into his body. He could feel his limbs tingling, his fingers and toes going numb. He had to get out of the frigid water fast or he wouldn't be able to move at all. And he definitely didn't want to be in the lake when the serpent decided to come back. Left with no choice, he grabbed a single oar floating nearby and swam toward Fred.

He reached the statue and clumsily heaved himself across it. Straddling Fred's chest, he rode him like a chubby surfboard, paddling frantically toward the beach, terrified he'd spot a pair of burning red eyes trailing him in the water. Fortunately, his luck held and he made it back before the serpent returned.

Half-frozen, he dragged Fred ashore and parked him at the water's edge. Then he flopped face-down in the dirt, breathing hard.

A shadowy figure emerged from the bushes and strode toward him. Tom tensed and reached for the cutlass, but abruptly realized it must have slipped away from him somewhere in the lake. The man moved forward, stopping only inches from his head. Tom angled his neck back and saw a booted foot. A *single* booted foot and a wooden peg leg. Relief poured through him.

Umbrey.

"Interesting vessel you got there, lad." Umbrey nodded toward Fred. "But if you judge a man by the ship he captains, I'd say you're in pretty rough shape."

"At least I came back alive."

"Ah. The first rule of sailing: Don't drown. Well done." Umbrey peered down at Tom. "Looks like you got a little wet, however."

"It's a wet lake."

"Aye. Most of them are."

Tom and his friends had dressed Fred to resemble a pirate, but Umbrey was the real deal. Peg leg, ruffled shirt, knee breeches, and a velvet blazer. His skin was weathered from the sun and his voice was low and deep—the kind of voice that could carry orders across the deck of a ship.

Tom was about to ask him what had brought him there when something occurred to him. He scanned the beach. "Hey. Where'd everybody go?"

"Mortimer was here a few minutes ago. Discovered they were missing from their beds and chased 'em all back to school."

Tom groaned and rolled over. Perfect. Just when he thought the night couldn't get any worse. He'd earned another demerit on Professor Lost's list.

"What happened to you?" Umbrey demanded.

"There's something in the water. An eel . . . a sea serpent. I don't know. It attacked me." He reached into his pocket for the rattle tip of the creature's tail, which he'd grabbed before heading for shore. He withdrew it and passed it to Umbrey.

"So that's the stink on you." Umbrey gave the tail a shake. "A folly. *Pholidae*, technically. Nasty creatures. Fortunately for you, they like to play with their food before they eat it. Gives a man a fighting chance." He looked at Tom. "How'd you know its weak spot was its rattle?"

"I didn't. I was aiming for its throat."

"Beginner's luck, eh?"

Wincing at the throbbing ache in his back, Tom slowly got to his feet. "Yeah, I feel real lucky."

"Watch your tongue, lad. Sarcasm is not becoming of a sailor."

Tom wanted to remind him that he wasn't a sailor at all, just a normal fourteen-year-old kid who'd discovered a world he'd never guessed existed, met a twin brother he'd never known he had, and learned that he had been born with the unique ability to make ancient maps come alive. A dubious skill. It had led to him being chased by an evil army, nearly torn apart by savage dogs, swarmed by dragons, and threatened by tribal warriors. Now he could add attacked by a sea serpent to the list. He would have mentioned that, but Umbrey wasn't the sympathetic type. He probably would have just accused him of whining.

So Tom turned his attention instead to removing his life vest and wringing the ice water from his shirt. When he finished he found Umbrey watching him, a curious expression on his face.

"You don't know then, do you?"

"Know what?"

"About follies. There are men who've devoted their entire lives to hunting these creatures." He held the tip of the folly's tail aloft and gave it a soft shake. "Just to claim this prize."

"*That thing?* Why?"

"Think, lad. What does the word *folly* mean?"

Tom vaguely recalled seeing it once on a vocabulary test. He dredged his memory. "I don't know . . . doing something foolish, I guess. Building something ridiculous. Acting without thinking or showing good sense."

"Aye. Like making a wish and not understanding the consequences."

"Right." Tom nodded, then froze as Umbrey's words slowly sank in. "Making a wish? You don't mean . . . "

"I do." He tossed the tail back to Tom. "Only the one who captures the serpent's rattle can make the wish, and only once. So think hard before using it, if you choose to use it at all."

If he chose to use it? *If?*

Wild elation surged through Tom, leaving him almost dizzy with excitement. A wish. His mind whirled as hundreds of greedy thoughts bombarded him at once. A million dollars. A private jet. Lifetime season passes for him and his friends to snowboard. His very own pro basketball team. How could he possibly narrow it down?

He stared down at the object nestled in his palm. Pinecone shaped, it looked like an enormous rattlesnake tail. He held it cautiously, half-expecting it to suddenly sprout a claw and change into something else. It didn't. In Umbrey's hands, the thing was gray, dead-looking. But the moment Tom had touched it, it pulsed with light, emitting a gentle heat that warmed his icy fingers. "You're serious, right? You're not joking. This is real?"

"I'm afraid so."

"No matter what I wish for, this rattle thing will make it come true?"

"Aye. Your wish will be granted, but always at a cost."

A distant alarm sounded in Tom's mind. He narrowed his eyes at Umbrey. "What do you mean, 'at a cost'?"

"Wishes are dangerous things. They can turn a man's life in a direction he never meant to go. Many a man who captured the rattle lived to regret it." Umbrey gestured toward the water's edge. "Might be best to just throw it back in the lake now, while you still can."

Throw it back? Absolutely not.

Tom wanted it. Even more than he'd wanted it when he'd snatched it out of the frigid water. Something about it had called to him. Now he understood why.

Forgetting the ugly viciousness of the creature itself, he focused on the glowing warmth and beauty of the rattle. It pulsed to a silent rhythm of its own, shifting from fiery crimson to deep orange to shocking pink. Amazing. He could stare at it for hours.

Umbrey watched him for a moment, then he let out a low sigh and shook his head. "Well, don't say I didn't warn you. But if you're determined to keep the blasted thing, get it out of my sight."

Tom reluctantly stashed the rattle in his pocket. Turning away, he lifted Fred upright and stuck him in the packed dirt like a tilting Statue of Liberty. As he did, he noted that Fred had earned a souvenir from the battle as well: a jagged white scar stood out across his cheek. It gave him a dashing, rugged, and distinctly pirate-like air—a vast improvement to his former geeky prep school self.

Umbrey looked at the statue and seemed to concur. He nodded approvingly. "Gives him a little character, doesn't it?"

"Lost won't like it."

"No, I expect not. But we've got bigger problems to worry about."

Thunder rumbled and jagged forks of lightening split the sky. The long, drifting shadows in the woods were thrown into stark silhouette. They shifted through the tree limbs, reaching toward Tom and Umbrey like long, skeletal fingers. Icy apprehension curled up Tom's spine.

His gaze shot back to Umbrey. "The Watch?" he asked.

Umbrey's expression sobered. His mouth tightened into a grim line. He gave a quick shake of his head. "Worse, I'm afraid."

Tom's stomach clenched. "Porter?" he asked. "Is he all right? What about Mudge and Willa?"

"They're fine—for the moment, at least." Umbrey reached into his velvet coat and withdrew a loosely bound parchment scroll. One dog-earred corner flapped in the breeze. By the glimmer of moonlight, Tom was able to make out the crude sketch of a compass, its four points stretching north, south, east, and west. A map.

Umbrey held the scroll aloft.

"We need you, Tom. Now."

CHAPTER THREE

DARK MAPS

An anticipatory thrill ran through Tom. His fingers itched to spread the map open and run his hands over the thick parchment. But before he could, a thrashing sound echoed from the path behind them and Professor Mortimer Lost emerged, carrying with him a candlelit lantern, an umbrella, and his ever-present book of demerits.

Headmaster Lost, the founder of the Lost Academy, was long limbed and painfully thin, as though his maker had originally intended to fashion a crane, but changed his mind at the last minute. Lost had sunken eyes, a long chin, and a beaked nose that was perfect for sniffing out trouble. His thin lips were turned down in a scowl of perpetual disapproval, as though he constantly expected to find grave failings with those around him.

Tom had an unfortunate habit of obliging him.

"Thomas Hawkins," Lost's voice was shrill and stern. "Your co-horts in this shameful misadventure have already been dealt with. They are spending the rest of this evening scrubbing the latrines. Perhaps that will remind them that the rules of this institution are to be obeyed. And as for you—" He gave a horrified gasp as he glanced over Tom's shoulder and spied Fred.

His expression made it abundantly clear that he didn't find

Fred's scar quite as dashing as Tom and Umbrey had.

He stormed down to the shoreline to better inspect the statue, then wheeled around and thrust a bony finger at Tom. "Apparently you are determined to pander to the delinquent streak in your character. Defacing the school mascot. Leaving the dormitory after lights out. Entering the lake although it is expressly forbidden." He paused, his frown deepening as he noted the wooden debris that littered the beach. "Do not tell me—"

"It wasn't entirely the boy's fault," Umbrey interrupted. "You've got a folly in your lake. It might have been a little bit rough on your boats."

"A *pholidae*? In my lake?" Lost's eyes grew wide, then narrowed in disgust. "Impossible. I just had the water fumigated."

"Er . . . about that . . . " Umbrey scratched the coarse stubble on his chin. "The beastie might have slipped in with me. One of my men thought he smelled something foul on the starboard side, but we were in a bit of a hurry, you know. Don't have time to worry about every little thing."

"Every little . . . " Lost echoed, fuming. "That is precisely the sort of carelessness I'd expect from you, Umbrey."

"Now, now, Morty—"

"Do *not* call me Morty. You needlessly infected my lake, and to what end? We've already discussed this. There will be no more unnecessary travel between the Five Kingdoms and this academy. Clearly the boy's not ready."

"Not ready?" Tom interrupted. "I've *been* there. I've been to the Five Kingdoms. If they need me, I'm ready to go there again."

"Ready?" The headmaster gave a dry cackle. "Preposterous. You are a brash and impetuous child. Driven by reckless impulse rather than intellect. Without further discipline you will only be a danger to yourself and those around you."

"Maybe that's because I'm supposed to be *there*, and not here," Tom suggested firmly.

"Nonsense," Lost huffed.

"But—"

"That will do, Mr. Hawkins." Lost drew himself up to his full height and sent Tom a frosty glare. "Character is not determined by *where* you are, but by *who* you are. You would do well to remember that."

Exactly the sort of thing Lost would say. Tom ground his teeth in frustration. Umbrey gave the scroll he carried an impatient shake. "Is there somewhere we can look at this?"

Lost glared at Tom for a moment longer, a look of sharp displeasure on his face. As the seconds ticked past, Tom caught his breath, thinking the headmaster was going to refuse Umbrey's request. Finally, however, Lost stomped the tip of his umbrella into the packed dirt of the beach and gave a curt nod.

"As you have gone to considerable lengths to bring that scroll here—infecting my lake in the process—I shall grant you the courtesy of seeing what it depicts. Do *not*, however," he continued, turning to send Tom a stern glare, "interpret this as a sign of my willingness to permit you to return to the Five Kingdoms."

Lost directed them to the boathouse. The heavy padlock, picked by Tom's friends, swung uselessly against the doors.

"Apparently Mr. Hawkins has seen to it that we don't have to trouble ourselves with the key. How very expedient."

They stepped inside. Perched on a dock at the edge of the lake, the boathouse was perpetually damp, drafty, and musty-smelling. Most of the boats hung suspended in mid-air, swaying and creaking as though rowed by ghosts. But one boat had been lowered for repairs. It rested upside down in the center of the room on raised planks, its battered wooden hull facing the ceiling.

Using it as a makeshift table, Umbrey spread the map across the weathered hull. Lost stepped forward to look at it, then gave a sharp gasp and spun around to glare at Umbrey.

"A *dark map*? *Here*? You've brought a dark map to my school? What could you possibly have been thinking?"

"I had no choice, Mortimer. Now bring that light here so we can see the blasted thing."

Lost hesitated for a moment, his face pinched in distaste, before reluctantly drawing the candlelit lantern he carried closer to the map.

The movement threw long flickering shadows into the corners of the room. Tom had lost track of the approaching storm, but at that moment the weather chose to reassert itself. Wind howled and torrents of rain pelted the roof. Although his wet clothes hadn't bothered him earlier, he now had to clench his jaw to keep his teeth from chattering from the cold.

An icy gloom seemed to seep through the cracks in the floor's planking, enveloping them all. It took him a moment to realize that the dark chill he felt wasn't coming from the violent storm, but from the map Umbrey had opened.

He stepped closer to get a better look.

It was an ugly thing. Dull and dirty, torn in places, with none of the gritty elegance or splashes of color that had marked his father's work. But then, his father had mapped ancient legends. This was primarily a nautical map.

The map bore no title, but Tom was familiar enough with the Five Kingdoms to recognize the Cursed Souls Sea. Aquat, a nation comprised of a long chain of islands, dominated the western edge. Beyond that were Bloody Bay, Skeleton Harbor, Hurricane Hell, and Tsunami Shores. The Island of Doom was snuggled between the Island of Death and the Island of Despair.

"Give it a go, lad."

Tom nodded, immediately understanding Umbrey's instruction. He lifted his hand and cautiously drew it above the map's surface.

The map came alive! It shuddered and heaved as the Cursed Souls Sea began to churn, changing the water from a wretched blue to an angry bile green. Riptides, waterspouts, and cross currents shook the map's surface. Writhing nests of *pholidae*

hissed and rattled their tails, enormous great white sharks circled a sinking ship as the desperate crew cried out for help, a jellyfish whipped its long, slimy tentacles upward as a school of prehistoric-looking flying fish leapt from the water and dove back into the map's churning sea.

Then, in a movement so fast Tom had no warning it was coming, a skeletal hand shot from the water and grabbed his wrist.

Tom yelped and jerked back his hand, but no matter how hard he tugged, he couldn't break the hold. Mostly bone and claw, the hand was not quite human, not quite animal, but something in between. The thing—whatever it was clung to it, searing his flesh like a burning hot vise.

As he watched in horror, a skeletal face slowly took shape beneath the water's surface. It peered up at him with an angry scowl, its teeth black and rotted, its watery eyes bloodshot, a grayish-green tinge to its peeling flesh.

Umbrey swore and grabbed Lost's lantern. He jerked the candle free and thrust the flame at the claw imprisoning Tom's wrist. The creature abruptly released him.

Tom staggered backward. His heart hammered wildly in his chest as he drew in great gulps of air. His gaze shot to the map, but the creature was gone. The map returned to its dull, dry state. There was no evidence of what he'd seen or felt. Nothing except the angry red welt that was beginning to form on his wrist.

"What was that?"

Umbrey and Lost exchanged a long, silent look. "I had hoped when the boy took the sword, we might be spared that particular calamity."

"What was that thing?" Tom pressed.

"They're known as scavengers, lad," Umbrey said. "The Cursed Souls Sea has been home to those nasty creatures for centuries. But now they're on the move."

"You're certain?" Lost asked. "It's not just—"

"There have been sightings."

"I see." Lost gave a curt nod. His narrow lips puckered, as though he were tasting Umbrey's words and finding them bitter. Moving with utmost care, he gently latched the lantern shut. "Well. So there you have it."

"Have what?" Tom said.

"Reckoning," Lost answered flatly. "The scavengers are a penance, Mr. Hawkins. Retribution for past sins. That creature . . . " His voice faded away as he stared blindly off into the dark corners of the boathouse. Tom could almost see the headmaster's thoughts whirling. Then Lost's gaze moved to Umbrey.

"The map," he said, pointing to the parchment. "I take it there may be a way to stop them?"

"Aye."

"The black book?"

Umbrey gave a reluctant nod. "I'm afraid it's our only chance."

Lost thought for a moment longer, then drew himself up.

His dark eyes burned with fiery righteousness. In the flickering candlelight, dressed as he was in his old-fashioned suit, he looked for a moment like a stock character in some ancient black-and-white movie. The avenging preacher facing down a horde of brash outlaws.

"Mr. Hawkins," he intoned, "you claim you are ready to return to the Five Kingdoms."

Tom jumped to attention. He gave a firm nod. "I am."

"Very well." Lost's keen gaze combed him over from head to foot. "Fools will tell you that there are infinite shades of gray in life. That the line between right and wrong can easily be blurred. Do not believe them. There is good and there is evil. That is all. You are about to discover that every action, every choice, every *wish*, has a direct and tangible consequence." He paused, his eyes boring into Tom's. "Do you understand me?"

"Yes, sir."

Satisfied, Lost turned to Umbrey. "I commend him into your care. I suspect the boy would like to return alive and unharmed. A reasonable request. This would be my preference, if it is at all possible."

"I can't make you any promises, Mortimer, given what we're up against, but I'll do my best." Umbrey rolled the map and returned it to the inner pocket of his frock coat. He turned to look at Tom. "Ready, lad?"

"Ready," Tom replied, though suddenly he wasn't quite as sure. He wanted a middle ground. Somewhere between Lost's dire warnings and Umbrey's devil-may-care attitude. But clearly that wasn't an option.

He followed Umbrey out of the building. The driving rain had lessened, diminishing to a soft sprinkle. In its place, a heavy fog enveloped the lake. As Tom watched, the mist parted, allowing him a glimpse of an enormous, old-fashioned sailing ship parked against the edge of the dock. He blinked, certain he had imagined it, but when he opened his eyes again it was still there.

Painted in gold on the side of the hull was the name

Purgatory. The ship shimmered in the moonlight, its billowing white sails almost ghostlike.

Lost studied the ship in silence, a faraway look in his eyes. In a tone that was almost wistful, he said, "She's a fine vessel, Umbrey."

"Aye, that she is." Umbrey joined Lost in admiring the ship. Then he gave a brisk nod and strode up the plank shouting orders to his crew. Tom moved to follow him.

"Mr. Hawkins."

He stopped and turned.

Lost stood on the dock, tightly clenching his book of demerits. His mouth worked silently, as though he was struggling to spit something out. Finally he managed, "Despite your wild and willful behavior, your presence at this academy is not completely intolerable. Try not to do anything idiotic and get yourself killed."

Tom stared at him in astonishment. Coming from the headmaster, that was almost a hug. He nodded. "Yes, sir."

He followed Umbrey aboard. Unlike Umbrey, who displayed a natural affinity for fine clothing, dressing in outrageous velvets and laces, his crew was comprised of a motley assortment of crude, rough, heavily armed men. To Tom, they looked more like a biker gang than a group of sailors. But he had seen them in action and their loyalty to their captain was unquestioned.

Working with the silent precision, they quickly had the *Purgatory* under way. The sails snapped, capturing the wind and propelling them forward on the lake's rolling surface. The deck pitched and rolled beneath his feet. Tom watched from the stern as Professor Lost faded into a small, insignificant speck.

Turning away, he joined Umbrey on the foredeck.

"Ah, there you are!" Umbrey said. "Nothing like the thrill of setting off on a new voyage. Isn't that right, lad?"

Tom grinned. He had never been aboard a ship before. But if this was what it was like, he could understand why men spent their lives at sea.

"Almost there," Umbrey continued. "It'll just be another minute now. But I'm afraid our landing might be a bit damp." He grabbed a shiny yellow hat and matching slicker from a nearby hook and slipped them on. He offered a similar getup to Tom.

"Uh, no thanks." It was bad enough that one of them looked like the guy on the fish stick box. He could handle a little water.

Umbrey shrugged. "Suit yourself."

Turning away, Tom peered into the distance, enjoying the gentle fanning of the breeze against his face, the light sprinkle of rain hitting his cheeks.

Then something occurred to him. He'd been so caught up in the thrill of the midnight sail, he hadn't paid attention to their trek across the water. He took into account the size of the ship and the speed at which they were traveling. Odd. They should have reached the end of the lake by now.

He realized with a jolt of surprise that he couldn't even *see* the end. None of the towering pines that rimmed the lake were visible. Instead, all he could make out ahead of them was shimmering darkness. The horizon was blacker than black, as though someone had punched a hole in the night sky. A gaping empty hole . . .

Then he heard it. Subtle at first, then stronger and stronger. The roar of water tumbling over a cliff. A roar so loud it sounded like an explosion.

"Steady, men!" Umbrey cried. "Keep her straight. Easy does it!"

Tom's mouth went dry. He'd seen it over and over, but he hadn't connected it. Hadn't believed it. Even though ancient maps all showed the same thing: ships falling off the edge of the earth. He had assumed it was a fantasy invented by cartographers. Proof of their ignorance of the curvature of the earth.

Reality hit him hard. *He'd* been the ignorant one. The earth did have an edge, and he was about to plummet over it. The sails snapped, the timbers creaked and groaned. The ship shuddered as though it was about to be split in two.

The *Purgatory* tipped, teetering over the vertical brink. Tom's stomach lurched as the horizon tilted, then swung out of view.

Umbrey shot him a grin. Anticipation gleamed in his eyes as he gripped the ship's rail.

"Hold on tight, lad. We're going in."

CHAPTER FOUR

REUNION

The *Purgatory* pitched forward, shooting head-first into a freefall. Absolute darkness enveloped them, leaving nothing but the ear-shattering roar of water. Tom's knees buckled. He scrambled for a hold but was too late. His feet slid out from under him, knocking him forward. His body slammed upside down against the rail as though he'd been caught in mid-somersault with his cheek pressed against the deck and his feet dangling in the air. He tried to right himself but gravity pinned him down and held him there, settling atop him like an invisible weight.

Just when it seemed their fall would never end, the ship abruptly righted. Unable to stop himself, Tom slid backward as the *Purgatory* landed with a tremendous splash. An enormous wave slammed the deck. Tom's clothing had just begun to dry after his plunge in the icy lake. Now it was plastered to his skin once again, soaked.

He coughed up water. Dazed, he blinked up at the night sky. Stars. There were stars in the sky again. Which meant they'd made it . . . somewhere.

Umbrey leaned over him, his scruffy face temporarily blocking Tom's line of vision. He slipped off his rain slicker and hat and hung them up. Then he grinned and rubbed his hands together. "Quite a ride, eh, lad?"

Tom had clenched his jaw to keep from screaming during their descent. Now he wrenched his teeth apart and asked, "Does that mean we're still alive?"

"Aye. Alive and then some. Nothing like a dip over the edge of the earth to get a man's blood pumping."

"Right," Tom groaned. He struggled to his feet and stood, gripping the rail for support, hating the way the ship pitched and swayed beneath him as it settled back into the water. He might have made it over the earth's edge, but clearly he'd left his stomach back at the Forbidden Lake.

"You look a little green around the gills, lad. Never fear, I'll make a sailor out of you yet."

"Uh, no thanks." He shot Umbrey a sideways glare. "Did you even *think* about warning me?"

"Warning you? Now where's the fun in that?"

"*Fun?* That was fun to you?"

"Course it was. Come now, where's your spirit? Your sense of adventure?" He looked at Tom, watching as rivulets of water ran down his body and gathered in a puddle at his feet. He motioned to a crewman. "Take him below and find him some dry clothes."

"Wait a minute," Tom protested. "Wait. First I need to know where—"

"That's an order, lad."

Tom looked from Umbrey to the burly crewman who waited to take him below decks. A thousand questions burned through his brain, but obviously Umbrey wasn't going to answer them until he cooperated. Biting back his impatience, he followed the crewman down a maze of ladders and passageways, moving deeper and deeper into the belly of the ship until they reached what appeared to be the crew's quarters.

Rows of empty hammocks hung from open rafters, swaying gently to the tidal rhythms. The crewman pulled out a dark chest. Flipped open the lid. Pointed inside.

"Um . . . got it. Thanks."

The crewman turned and walked away, leaving Tom alone. He stripped off his sopping wet sneakers, jeans, and Lost Academy T-shirt, exchanging them for a pale linen shirt, dark green tunic, brown woolen pants, and a pair of rugged leather boots. No buttons, zippers, or snaps. All of the clothing laced and tied. He struggled with them for a few frustrating minutes. Finally satisfied his pants wouldn't end up around his ankles when he moved, he rejoined Umbrey above decks.

When he'd gone below, there had been nothing but twinkling stars overhead and the glossy blackness of a vast sea. But in his absence, the *Purgatory* had left the broad sea and entered a channel that carried them inland. Flickering in the distance were dozens, perhaps hundreds, of tiny lights.

"Where are we?"

"Approaching Divino."

An anticipatory thrill shot through him. Divino—center of the Five Kingdoms, Keegan's stronghold. After months of waiting, after long nights wondering how Porter, Willa, and

Mudge were faring, he was finally back.

The shrill peal of a bell echoed across the deck, temporarily dampening his excitement. Tom winced and frowned at Umbrey. He thought that particular system of torture had been left behind at the Lost Academy.

"Bells? Really?"

"Duty watch," Umbrey replied with an indifferent shrug. "Keeps order. Only way to run a ship." He peered off into the distance, then straightened. "Look sharp, lad. We're here."

The enormous wooden gates of the walled city came into view. The last time Tom had been in Divino he'd had to scale the walls and fight his way inside. Now Umbrey grabbed a lantern and held it aloft. The lantern had been fitted at the front with a black face that covered the flame. Umbrey slid the door up and down—a signal code, Tom assumed, watching him. Sure enough, the guard stationed in the gate tower signaled back, then the heavy iron bar lifted and the gates that protected the channel slowly groaned open.

As they sailed between them, Tom noted the faint outline of a glowing red eye, symbol of Keegan's army of vicious thugs, was still visible on the gate's wooden surface. Though a dark stain had been applied over it, the eye had not been entirely blotted out. A chill ran through him at the sight of it. He couldn't help but wonder if the unsuccessful attempt to obliterate the eye was some sort of omen, a dark portent of things to come.

He pushed the thought away as the *Purgatory* drifted downriver and docked. He followed Umbrey across the ship's gangway. They stepped onto what might once have been a bustling wharf. Now, however, the ships, warehouses, and wagons all looked deserted. Everything Tom saw had been cast aside, abandoned in a disturbing, unnatural way—sacks of grain left untended, casks of wine tipped over, bolts of fabrics rolling about in the mud and muck. It was as though whoever owned the goods had simply dropped them there in a hurry and fled.

"What happened here?" he asked, following Umbrey ashore.

Umbrey gave him a quick, side-long glance. "Best keep your voice down. You'll want to listen now."

"Listen? For what?"

Umbrey's expression darkened. "Trust me, lad. You'll know it when you hear it."

When Tom had last left Divino, it had been in the middle of a great celebration. That was a stark contrast to what he saw now. Groups of people cowered in doorways and alleyways, huddled around small rings of fire. Others gathered beneath lit torches. Several buildings had been stripped of wood, suggesting fuel for the fires was in short supply. Tom tried to make sense of it. People hovered near the flames as though in desperate need of heat, though the night was mild.

There was no sound, no noise at all save the soft echo of Umbrey's peg leg hitting the cobbledstoned streets. Nothing else. Just eerie silence. As they walked down the street, Tom could feel their every movement watched, analyzed. Like mist in the moonlight, fear seeped through the alleyways, settled over his skin and clogged his throat. Soon even he was convinced something dark and threatening waited around the next corner.

At last they reached a broad stone building. Djembe warriors guarded the entrance. The iridescent chain mail they wore over their chests shimmered in the flickering torchlight. Their presence should have been reassuring, but somehow it wasn't.

A lone, hooded figure detached itself from the group of warriors. Tall and lean, the figure moved with a long, purposeful stride that Tom recognized at once.

Porter.

Tom and Porter didn't look like brothers. They definitely

didn't look like twins. Porter had fair skin, ice blue eyes, and pale blond hair that brushed his shoulders—a stark contrast to Tom's dark complexion, brown eyes, and closely-cropped chestnut hair.

They didn't act like brothers, either. Tom tended to be impulsive and emotional; Porter was rational and distant. Tom took wild chances, Porter calculated odds.

Most importantly, they didn't *feel* like brothers, at least to Tom. More like two strangers who'd been plunged into a situation where they'd had to depend upon each other to survive. As far as he could tell, that was their only bond.

Tom had tried to picture a reunion with Porter. He'd never quite been able to imagine what that would feel like. Now he realized why. They still didn't know each other.

That fact was made even more obvious as they studied each other in silence, caught in a state of clumsy awkwardness. Tom tried to come up with a suitable greeting. A hug wasn't even in the realm of possibility. Shaking hands seemed too formal.

Porter solved the dilemma by giving him a cool nod. "Hey," he said.

Tom nodded back. "Hey."

Watching them, Umbrey chortled. "Careful, lads. You'll embarrass me with that gushing display of emotion."

Porter gave a small, half-smile. It vanished as a low howl sounded in the distance. His face went still and his hand moved to the blade tucked into his belt. His eyes darted to the shadows, seeking out the darkened corners.

"Easy, lad. It's just a dog. Besides, you know that knife won't do you any good."

Porter relaxed his grip on his blade. His expression sheepish, he gave a quick nod. "Right. I know that." He let out a long, steadying breath, then looked at Tom. "C'mon. We haven't much time. Willa and Mudge are waiting inside."

Tom shot a questioning glance at Umbrey. His brother was not the type to easily spook. Porter's nervousness made him even more uneasy.

He didn't have long to dwell on it. Umbrey nodded to the warrior guards, who opened the door and ushered them inside. Tom quickly gained his bearings. They stood in a large, open room, complete with a judge's bench, witness stand, and jury box. There were benches for the spectators. A courthouse of sorts, he surmised.

"Tom!"

Willa grabbed him and wrapped him in a tight hug. Mudge repeated the gesture. For a moment, everything was good. Better than good—exactly the way he'd hoped things would be when he returned to the Five Kingdoms. No abandoned wharfs or sinister shadows lurking in the streets. No hesitation or weirdness at being reunited. Just the hugs and smiles of old friends getting together again. Finally they released each other and stepped back.

"You came," Mudge said. "I wasn't sure . . . "

"Of course I'm here. Umbrey said you needed me."

Mudge nodded and chewed his lower lip. Unable to meet Tom's eyes, he looked away. Though just ten years old, the boy looked weighed down with worry.

Tom's gaze moved to Willa. She dressed in simple wool clothing and styled her long, pale-brown hair in a heavy braid. Tom had remembered that she was pretty. He just hadn't remembered *how* pretty. Or how unassuming she was about it. She was one of those girls who didn't try to be attractive—a fact that made her even more attractive. But as he looked closer, he noticed the shadows under her hazel eyes, suggesting she hadn't slept in days.

He frowned. It didn't make sense. Something wasn't right. They had defeated Keegan. They'd recovered Salamaine's sword, brought Keegan's reign to an end, and installed Mudge as rightful heir and ruler of the Five Kingdoms. The battle was over. Or at least he'd thought it was.

Then he considered what he'd seen since he'd left the *Purgatory*. The darkened streets. The silence and fear.

"What's out there? What's everyone so afraid of?"

"They haven't told you yet?" Willa said, her face pained. "You don't know about Salamaine's Curse? About the scavengers?"

Tom shook his head. "Tell me."

Porter dragged a hand through his hair. "It'll take too long to explain—"

"Then skip the explanations. Just give me the facts."

Tom could almost feel his brother's impatience. But instead of arguing the point, Porter gave a curt nod and collected his thoughts. "When Salamaine was king, he made a mistake. A bad mistake. As a result, hundreds of innocents lost their lives." He stopped, shook his head, and corrected himself. "Or rather, *almost* lost their lives. For they didn't die, not completely. They came back from the dead to hunt Salamaine, seeking revenge for their deaths."

They came back from the dead? Tom's mind shot to the creature he'd seen on the dark map in the boathouse. "Scavengers," he said, as though testing the word aloud. "I saw one. It came to life on the map of the Cursed Souls Sea."

Porter nodded again. "For centuries the scavengers were trapped in that sea. But not anymore. We fought off the first wave, but more are on their way here—hordes of them."

"It's my fault," Mudge said. He ran his fingers lightly along the hilt of the Sword of Five Kingdoms, which he wore tucked into his belt. "When I woke Salamaine's blade, I woke the scavengers. They want to avenge their deaths. That's why they come."

"Until we stop them," Umbrey interjected, placing a reassuring hand on Mudge's shoulder.

"How do we do that?" Tom asked.

"The Black Book of Pernicus." Umbrey withdrew the map from the inner pocket of his coat rapping the scroll of parchment against his palm. "It's the only way."

Tom's confusion must have been obvious, for Willa added, "Pernicus created the scavengers. It's said the answer to destroying the creatures lies within the pages of his book."

"Then what are we waiting for?" Tom said. "If we have the map, let's go."

Willa shifted uncomfortably, her gaze sliding from Umbrey to Porter.

Porter cleared his throat. "Technically," he said, "the map doesn't belong to us. It will only reveal the book if the map's owner wants us to find it."

Tom frowned. "Who owns it?"

Another heavy pause, this one broken by Umbrey. "He's waiting below," he replied gruffly. He gave the map another sharp rap. "All right, then. Enough talk. Let's get this done."

He ushered them toward a set of stone steps that led to a lower level. A basement dungeon of some sort. The rock walls felt dank and damp, wet to the touch. There were no windows. The only light in the room was provided by flickering torches, encased in wrought iron sconces on the walls.

The room had been designed to hold prisoners before trial, Tom guessed. Rather than partitioning the space into a series of small cells, the jail encompassed the entire basement. It was one huge, open cell. Stone walls on three sides, stone floors, iron bars across the front. It could easily house dozens of men. Likely, it normally did. But at the moment, it held only one prisoner.

Keegan.

A CURSED SWORD

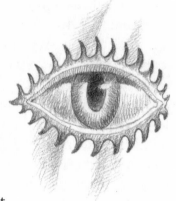

The door to Keegan's cell was open. Tom hesitated on the threshold, feeling as if he were about to enter the lair of some lethal, predatory animal. Though Keegan did nothing to acknowledge them, Tom was certain he was alert to their every move. He hung back for a moment, cautiously taking the man in.

Keegan wore dark wool pants, a brocade vest, plum shirt, and expensive black boots. A fur cape was dramatically draped over his shoulders, and his hair and goatee were immaculately groomed. If not for the overwhelming threat of menace he exuded, some might have considered him darkly handsome. At the very least, he looked like a rich, powerful nobleman.

Tom tore his gaze away from Keegan to sweep the rest of the room. It was unlike any jail cell he'd ever seen. Gilt mirrors, thick animal skin rugs, finely crafted table and chairs, shelves of books, and an enormous four poster bed with a rich silk coverlet. The opulence was unnerving. The only indication he could find that Keegan was a prisoner, rather than an illustrious guest, was the iron chain that looped from his ankle to a peg in the wall.

Despite the lateness of the hour, Keegan sat at a candlelit table laden with fine china and crystal goblets. A bloody slab of meat filled his plate. He slowly sliced and chewed his food, dabbing his mouth with a napkin, sipping his wine. He seemed perfectly indifferent to their presence, a rich aristocrat not to be bothered with the petty comings and goings of his jailors.

"Careful you don't choke on that," Umbrey said. "What an unseemly end to your reign. The mighty Keegan died in jail choking on a bone."

Keegan looked up. His lips curled into in a small smile. "Ah. My good friend, Umbrey. So nice of you to visit." He set his knife and fork aside and pushed back his plate. "I always did appreciate your humor. I must remember to make certain you're smiling when I post your head on a pike outside the gates of my new palace."

"An impressive threat for a man with a chain around his leg."

Keegan gave a royal shrug. The chain rattled across the stone floor as he leaned back in his chair and crossed his legs. "Do forgive the noise. My latest accessory. Meant to keep me humble, I suppose. Wallow in my disgrace and all that." He made a bored motion with his hand, then idly drew one long, yellow, talon-like nail along the rim of his goblet. "I see you've brought your little friends with you. What a rare treat."

Porter stepped forward. "You know why we're here."

Keegan leveled Porter with a long, silent gaze. "You know why we're here, *sire*," he corrected.

Porter didn't speak, but only continued to glare at him.

Keegan released a forlorn sigh. "Youth today. No respect." He shook his head, then continued, "Of course I know why you came. Even in here I can feel it bubbling and brewing outside— such glorious tension and anxiety, such utter terror." His dark eyes shimmered. "Scavengers. They're on their way."

"Unless we stop them," Porter said.

"With *my* map," Keegan countered. His lips twisted in a smile of dark satisfaction. "My people need me."

"Your people despise you," retorted Willa.

"Are you so certain of that?"

Willa brought up her chin. "Yes."

Keegan shook his head. "How painfully naïve. Permit me to enlighten you as to the way the world works. The good people of Divino may cringe in their homes as my army marches triumphantly through the streets, but they allow it. Why? Because everyone has food on the table and the wagons run on time. They *need* me."

A map of the Five Kingdoms filled one entire wall of his cell. Keegan rose and moved to stand beside it, his chain dragging behind him. Divino was at the heart of the map. The remaining four lands were equidistant from the center, spread out like the jagged claws of a crab: Aquat, an island chain bordering the Cursed Souls Sea; Incendia, a land ringed by fiery volcanoes; Terrum, a dense, jungle-like expanse of thick forests; and finally, Ventus, an icy mountain range beset by frosty winds.

"What did you think would happen?" Keegan asked. "You'd put a child on the throne, ask everyone to play nice, and all the problems in the Five Kingdoms would magically disappear? I'm afraid it doesn't work that way." He drew his hand across the map. "Five kingdoms. Each with its own self-interest. I maintained *order*. There is a delicate balance to it all, of which you know nothing."

"Then I will learn," Mudge replied, his voice small but defiant.

"Will you? Tell me then, what makes a good ruler?"

"Courage, honor, integrity, loyalty."

Keegan gave a harsh laugh. He brought his fingers against

his thumb in what was apparently the international symbol for *yak-yak-yak*.

"No. That is precisely wrong. There are only two kinds of people in the world. Those who inflict pain, and those who suffer it. Allow me to demonstrate."

He returned to his seat at the table and leaned back, assuming a posture of cool elegance. It was just an ordinary chair, but something about Keegan's pose made it seem regal, as though he was sitting on a throne. He turned his focus to the outer guard. A dark, simmering heat burned in his eyes. The guard stiffened, shifting nervously from foot to foot.

"Why is my glass empty?" Keegan said.

The guard sprang to action. He rushed to refill Keegan's glass, apologizing profusely for the delay. He bowed and retreated up the stone staircase and out of the room.

Satisfied, Keegan took a sip of wine. He turned to Tom and his friends. "Fear. Fear is how one controls."

Tom shook his head. "Temporarily, maybe. But not for long."

"Is that so?" Returning his attention to the table, he reached for a plate of tiny, decadent cakes, drenched in what looked like chocolate glaze, and popped one into his mouth. He chewed and swallowed, then took his time licking the rich glaze from his fingers.

"Why do you think the citizens of Divino allow me to live in such luxury?" he asked, gesturing around his cell. "Because they dare not displease me, that's why. I am temporarily inconvenienced, not vanquished. They know it."

"Your own men have deserted you," Porter answered flatly. "The Watch has fled."

"No. They have not fled. They simply await my command." He leaned back in his chair, staring in satisfaction at Tom and Porter. "Just as *the mapmaker's sons* have come to serve me."

Tom looked at Umbrey, then shifted his gaze to Porter, Willa, and Mudge. They all looked pale, tense. Defenseless against Keegan. This wasn't right. They had *defeated* him.

But they still needed him. The bitterness of it lodged in his throat.

A cruel smile played about Keegan's lips. "Ironic, isn't it? You thought the battle was over when you gained that pretty sword, yet it's only just begun." Thoroughly enjoying himself, he leaned forward, saying in a dramatic whisper, "A cursed sword. Such a shame. If only you'd known."

"The blade still had the power to destroy you," Porter shot back.

"Destroy me?" Keegan's dark brows shot upward. "My dear boy, do I look destroyed? All you've done is waste my time. An offense you'll pay dearly for, I can assure you, but not until I've availed myself of you and your brother's unique gift."

"What do you want, Keegan?" Umbrey said with a growl.

Keegan shook his head, making a *tsk*ing sound with his tongue. "So righteous, all of you. Salamaine's curse created the scavengers, yet here you are, coming to me to save you from them." He rose and looked at Umbrey. "You brought the map?"

Umbrey removed the rolled scroll from his coat.

With a careless swipe of his arm, Keegan cleared the table, sending the china and crystal crashing to the floor. He grabbed the map of the Cursed Souls Sea and spread it across the newly vacant surface.

"Read it," Keegan commanded. "Show me the Black Book of Pernicus."

Not about to take orders from Keegan, Tom looked at Umbrey. He gave a curt nod. "Do it, lads."

Porter stationed himself at one end of the table. Tom wordlessly followed suit, taking the opposite end. Their eyes met, and together they placed their fingers on the edges of the map.

Thick clouds of silver mist rose from the map. The sea began to froth and foam. Waves rose and crashed. Beneath the surface of the ocean, shadowy creatures slithered and writhed. Tom's stomach clenched. He broke out in a fine sweat. Rather than the euphoria he normally felt when touching a map, he felt nauseous, dizzy. Seasick. As though the floor beneath him pitched and rolled.

As he watched, a stark outcropping of rocks rose from the depths of the Cursed Souls Sea. The rocks shifted, growing larger and broader until they became a barren island. The scattered remains of an ancient city spread across the island. Dominating the northern end was a towering fortress surrounded by barrel-chested guards, all of whom brandished glistening scimitar swords.

"Arx," Keegan breathed. "It does exist."

Within the fortress was a single black book, floating in mid-air. From the corner of his eye, Tom saw Keegan remove a gold key from his pocket and place it on the map. The pages of the book fluttered open.

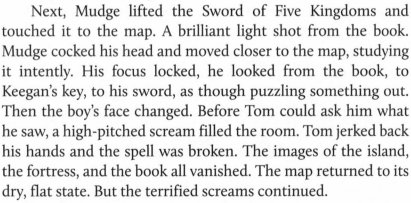

Next, Mudge lifted the Sword of Five Kingdoms and touched it to the map. A brilliant light shot from the book. Mudge cocked his head and moved closer to the map, studying it intently. His focus locked, he looked from the book, to Keegan's key, to his sword, as though puzzling something out. Then the boy's face changed. Before Tom could ask him what he saw, a high-pitched scream filled the room. Tom jerked back his hands and the spell was broken. The images of the island, the fortress, and the book all vanished. The map returned to its dry, flat state. But the terrified screams continued.

He glanced at Porter. His brother had gone even paler than usual. So had Willa.

Another scream echoed through the room. It took Tom a moment to realize the sounds weren't coming from the map at all—or from anywhere in the basement cell. The panicked screams came from somewhere beyond the courthouse.

Then he heard something else. Umbrey had told him he would know it when he heard it. He'd been right, for this was a sound he knew he would remember for the rest of his life. A low, steady, desperate moan. The sound of hunger and pain and rage all coiled into one. An animal-like howl with a human edge.

Above their heads, the door to the courthouse crashed open—or possibly was knocked off its frame—impossible to tell which from where he stood. Tom's gaze shot to the ceiling. The slow, heavy shuffle of feet echoed overhead. It sounded as though someone—or maybe a group of people—had entered the courtroom above them. But the sounds they made weren't normal. He heard grunts and groans, followed by staggering, stumbling footsteps. As though whoever was up there was dragging something very heavy behind them.

Willa's eyes widened in horror. She grabbed Mudge and pulled him protectively toward her.

"We were supposed to have time," Porter said, panicked. "I heard the reports. They were last seen crossing Mumdai. They're not supposed to be here yet."

"Release me!" Keegan cried, pulling at the chain that secured his ankle. "I won't die like this! Not ripped apart by scavengers."

"Shut up!" barked Umbrey.

"Release me now or you'll all die—all of you! You saw the map. You need me! You can't open the book without my key!"

Mudge tore away from Willa and ran to the outer cell wall. He grabbed the thick iron key that unlocked Keegan's shackle and rushed back to the cell.

Porter blocked his way. "*No*. You can't let him go. Think of everything he's done."

In that instant, Mudge looked far older than his years. He met Porter's eyes. "I *know* what he's done. But he's right. The book would be useless without him." He turned to Keegan. "If I release you, you will accompany us as our prisoner."

"Fine. The key. *Now*."

"Swear it."

"Yes, yes, I swear. *Now give me that key!*"

Mudge tossed it to him.

Keegan caught it and freed himself. He shook off his chain, then reached for a torch and held it aloft. His eyes met Tom's. "Marrick's chosen," he said, his lips curled back in a sneer. "This horror was not created by me, but by your good and brave King Salamaine. Look. Look what he has wrought."

Tom looked.

The creature from the map, but much, much worse. Now there were more of them. Too many to count. Filthy, battered, and bruised, their clothing hung in tatters from their skeletal frames as they stumbled down the rough stone steps, pushing and shoving past each other to gain entrance to the basement cell. They moved with their claw-like hands stretched out in front of them, their feet lurching unevenly, monotone grunts and growls issuing from their throats.

Odd clumps of hair sprung from their scalps. Their skin was gray and peeling, their lips rotted off to reveal blackened gums and tangled teeth. The putrid stench of rotting flesh hovered in the air around them.

The word *zombie* flew into Tom's brain and lodged there. But rather than provide him with the shot of adrenaline he desperately needed to jolt himself into action, the realization of what he was facing froze him in place. He couldn't move, couldn't breathe. His feet felt cemented to the cold stone floor. *Run! Get away, now!*

He cast a panicked glance around the room. The rush of adrenaline he'd hoped for finally came, but it was too late. The stairs, their only exit, were blocked by the creatures. There was no where to run, no other way out. They were trapped inside.

CHAPTER SIX

SCAVENGERS

Scavengers. Zombies. The names might not be the same, but the creatures were. As far as Tom could tell, there was no difference between them. But as they drew closer, he noted that one feature was altogether unlike the zombies he'd seen on TV and in movies,.

Scavengers' eyes were not vacant. They were not dull or glassy. Instead, they burned with lethal fury. Deadly rage. They might be slow and unsteady, but these were thinking, angry beings.

He watched the scavengers stumble down the stone steps. His initial instinct, born of both fear and repulsion, was to draw back into Keegan's cell until help arrived. Cowardly, maybe, but it would keep them alive. He shook off his terror long enough to reach for the cell door and slam it shut, but Umbrey stopped him.

"They'll only rip the bars out. Best we fight them directly."

Rip the bars out? Iron bars lodged in stone?

The creatures possessed that sort of strength? The desperation of their situation quickly sunk in.

Tom shot a glance at his brother. Porter lifted a torch from an iron sconce in the wall and passed it to him. Umbrey armed himself in a like manner, as did Willa. A dim ray of understanding lit a corner of Tom's brain. That explained all the small fires he'd seen when he'd first arrived in Divino.

Keegan held his torch before him, his posture that of an experienced fencer beginning a match. Watching him, Tom repressed a choked laugh. It wasn't Keegan's action that amused him, or even his pose, but the absurdity of facing an enemy so terrifying that they were actually aligned with Keegan, rather than fighting against him. A minute ago he would have sworn that was impossible.

The scavengers shuffled closer.

Goosebumps shot up the back of Tom's neck. His heart pounded furiously within his chest. The creatures' stench, a foul mixture of death and disease and rotted fish, soured the air, making it almost impossible to breathe.

Mudge brought up the Sword of Five Kingdoms. Liquid relief poured through Tom. He'd forgotten Mudge's sword. A sword so powerful it had taken out Keegan's army with one swift stroke. He watched as Mudge raised the sword above his head. They were saved. They'd get out of there, regroup, and—

Mudge swung at the scavengers. A blast of fiery white heat shot from the end of the blade . . . and went *through* the scavengers. It didn't even slow them down.

"Circle up! Everyone, now!"

Tom didn't know who the voice belonged to. He didn't care. He simply obeyed. They formed a tight knot, their shoulders brushing. The scavengers stumbled closer, desperately clawing and grabbing at them.

One scavenger in particular seemed determined to get Tom. She was old, tall, and skeletal, with frizzy red hair and dark brown eyes. If not for the strips of flesh peeling from her cheeks, she would have been a dead ringer for his algebra teacher. She tore through Tom's tunic with her sharp nails. He jabbed her in the eye with his torch. She backed off, but not enough, continuing to hiss and claw her way closer.

Using their torches to keep the scavengers at arm's length, they inched across the floor. After what seemed like forever, (though it probably took no longer than ten minutes) Tom and his friends reached the stairs. They slowly crept upward, thrusting their fire in the creatures' faces to keep them at bay. Finally Tom reached the top of the staircase. He staggered backward, followed by Porter, Willa, and Mudge. Umbrey and Keegan spilled out into the courtroom after them.

Porter slammed shut the heavy wooden door that led to the basement cell and threw down the iron bar that locked it. Tom, dragging in a deep, ragged breath, lifted his torch and swung it in a slow circle, sending flickering shadows into the darkened corners of the room. No scavengers—at least, not at the moment.

Outside, the quiet night had splintered like glass, shattering into a scene of utter pandemonium. Swishing arcs of firelight cut through the air like flaming swords. Dark silhouettes showed a few people fleeing, others fighting. Empty wagons careened through the streets, pulled by teams of wild-eyed horses.

A deep thud sounded on the door they'd just latched. The scavengers were right behind them. Within minutes, perhaps seconds, they'd have the door ripped off its hinges.

"No!"

He heard Willa's sharp cry and whirled around to see Keegan jerk Mudge toward him. Holding his torch aloft in one hand, Keegan locked his opposite arm across the boy's chest. He pressed a small, sharp knife beneath the boy's chin. When they'd first entered his cell, Tom had watched Keegan cut his meat. It hadn't occurred to him to wonder where his knife had gone. Now he knew.

Holding Mudge against him like a shield, Keegan edged toward the courthouse door. "The mapmaker's sons," he sneered. "The Hero Twins. You want to save the Five Kingdoms? Bring me the Black Book of Pernicus. You have three days. If you don't return, I'll assume you're dead. A nuisance, but I can make other adjustments."

"Let him go!" Willa shrieked. "He released you! You gave him your word!"

"*My word?!*" Keegan gave a shout of laughter. "My dear girl, you have just learned a very valuable lesson. Never underestimate your opponent."

"He won't hurt me," Mudge said. "The book's worthless unless Keegan and I are together. He knows it."

"Clever child." Keegan shot a glance over his shoulder to check the street. Seeing it was clear, he shoved Mudge away from him, sending him sprawling onto the floor. "Three days!" he said, and then he was gone, disappearing into the chaos of the night.

Porter shot forward to follow him, but Umbrey caught his arm. "Let him go."

"Let him go?! You'd let Keegan escape?"

"One battle at a time, lad. Mudge is right. He won't go far if he thinks there's a chance he can get his hands on that book."

Porter shook his head, his face wracked with frustration. "But—"

A heavy thud sounded against the basement door and the upper hinge flew off. Four pairs of ragged gray arms and twisted, claw-like hands shoved through the crack.

"The *Purgatory*," Umbrey urged. He peered out the door,

47

and seeing their way was clear, ushered them out into the night.

Tom still wasn't convinced. He hesitated, torn between taking off after Keegan or following Umbrey's orders. Umbrey didn't give him a chance to debate the matter. He shoved him toward the docks.

"*Now*, or we'll miss the tide—if we haven't already."

They set off into the night. The moon hung low in the sky, giving them ample light by which to see. Tom would have preferred dimness and shadows. Instead he could make out the face of each scavenger, every withered claw, bashed-in skull, and oozing limb.

Umbrey led them through the chaotic streets. Even with a wooden leg, the man moved fast. But then, they were all moving fast. Yet they couldn't quite move fast enough. It seemed that for every scavenger they avoided, two more lurched into their path. Finally, gasping and out of breath, they made it back to the docks and staggered to a horrified stop.

The *Purgatory* was under siege.

Scavengers clung to the hull like leeches. They scuttled up the masts, staggered across the deck, swung from the sails, and crowded onto the gangway. They moaned and grunted in murderous excitement, their eyes burning with feverish intensity.

Umbrey's men pitched the scavengers overboard, but the creatures wouldn't give up. They hit the water with a splash and flailed about, then seemed to gather their wits for a second attack. Dripping algae and seaweed, they crawled back up the hull and slipped through the ship's rail to advance again.

Umbrey released an outraged roar and charged into the middle of the fray. Wielding his torch like a club, he swung his arm back and forth, single-handedly making his way across the gangway. "Thought you'd come aboard my ship, did you?" he muttered as he sent the scavengers tumbling into the murky water below. "Not a chance, you slimy skinned, rotten-lipped, bug-eyed monsters."

Glancing over his shoulder, he bellowed orders to his crew.

Tom heard things like "Raise anchor! Throw the lines!" and "Bring the mizzen sail about!" Words that were gibberish to him, but clearly meant for the crew to get the ship moving. *Fast.*

They raced across the plank, Porter directly behind Umbrey, then Willa and Mudge, with Tom pulling up the rear. His friends jumped aboard. Tom was seconds from leaping onto the deck when a shrill scream pulled him up short. The naked desperation in the cry sent a chill up his spine. He wheeled about and peered into the surrounding chaos.

In the flickering light he made out a young woman who stood with her back pressed against a wall, feebly swinging a torch to keep a group of scavengers at bay. Two small, terrified children clung to her skirts.

Guessing his intent, Porter made to grab him and shove him aboard. "Don't," he shouted. "You'll never make it back!"

Tom brushed him off and flew down the gangway.

"Tom!" his brother roared. "Get back here! There's no time!"

The rest of his words were a blur. Tom reached the woman and swung his torch. It landed on the back of the largest scavenger in the group, lighting up his tattered shirt with a satisfying crackle of flame. The scavenger fell back, rolling on the ground, hissing and howling, clawing at air. Tom slashed his way through the rest of the group, pushing them back.

But there were too many. With a surge of horror, Tom realized he'd underestimated their number. As he fought one creature, another reached out to grab him. Its bony, claw-like hand locked around his wrist. Tom gave a yelp of pain. The scavenger's claw seared into his flesh, as unyielding as a band of hot iron.

The creature gave a grunt of satisfaction. It opened its rotted mouth and leaned closer. Strings of slime dripped from its blackened teeth. Tom swung his torch around, but another scavenger knocked it from his grasp.

His heart slammed against his chest as he braced himself for the bite.

Then, from the corner of his eye, a flash of flame.

Porter drove his torch into the creature's arm. The scavenger shrieked and released Tom. It staggered backward, allowing Tom just enough room to dive for his torch. He brought it up and swung it wide, standing shoulder-to-shoulder with Porter as they faced off against the scavengers. The woman took up a position beside them, thrusting her meager flame at the creatures as her children cowered behind her skirts.

The frantic beat of horses' hooves and the clatter of wooden wheels against the cobblestoned street blasted at Tom from his right. He turned to see a wagon bearing down on them at full speed. The driver, holding the horses' reins in one hand and an enormous flaming torch in the other, careened through the mob of scavengers, temporarily scattering them.

The woman nearly sagged to the ground in relief. Her husband, Tom guessed. Reaching behind her, she grabbed one child, then the other, depositing them in the back of the wagon. Once satisfied her children were safe, she leapt aboard.

The man looked at Tom and Porter. "Quickly!" he bellowed, "Get in!"

Porter gave a firm shake of his head. "No. *Go*."

The man looked ready to argue, but a guttural moan from the scavengers, who were lumbering back to their feet, changed his mind. His mouth tightened into a thin, grim line. "God be with ye," he muttered. He gave the reins a savage jerk. The horses reared, then bolted off into the night.

Tom and Porter didn't waste any time. They shot toward the docks. The *Purgatory* was still there. Barely. As they watched, the ship pulled away from the dock. The plank—along with the horde of scavengers piled upon it—tumbled into the watery channel below, landing with a resounding splash.

"Jump!" bellowed Umbrey.

Jump? Over scavenger-infested water onto a moving ship?

Insane. Tom cut a glance at his brother. Nothing but intense resolve showed on Porter's face. He was actually going to do it. Reluctant admiration found its way into Tom's assessment of Porter. Then something occurred to him. Maybe Porter wasn't *braver*, maybe he was just quicker at grasping their situation. Maybe his courage sprang from the fact that he recognized something Tom hadn't yet.

There was no other way aboard.

Porter picked up speed, gaining momentum for the leap. Tom matched his pace. Then his foot tangled with a length of rope obscured by shadows. He pitched forward. Rather than jumping for the ship, he staggered awkwardly and teetered at the end of the dock, nearly tumbling into the murky water below.

Beside him, Porter leapt. His brother sailed over the channel . . . and missed the *Purgatory's* deck. He slammed face-first into the hull and grabbed hold of the ship's barnacle-laden side. It was the barest of holds, but it was enough. Umbrey's men grabbed him and hauled him up, unceremoniously tossing him on deck like a sack of grain.

Tom's relief that Porter had made it aboard dissolved as his own predicament hit him.

He'd missed the boat. Literally.

The *Purgatory* was coasting out to sea without him.

CHAPTER SEVEN

BEYOND

THE

LOCKED GATES

Panic coursed through Tom. He judged the distance between the ship and the dock. Too far. He could jump, but he'd never make it. Not now. Not when the vessel was picking up speed. He scanned the wharf. No nearby boat he could use to row out to the *Purgatory*—not that rowing through scavenger-infested water struck him as the brightest of ideas.

Most likely they'd overtake him before he got anywhere near Umbrey and his crew. Indecision froze him in place. He couldn't go forward, he couldn't go back. But neither could he just stand there.

A guttural hiss sounded just over his shoulder, reinforcing that point. He jerked around to see a horde of scavengers lurching toward him, their skeletal arms stretched out as though hoping to wrap him in their ghoulish embrace.

That got him moving. Keeping parallel with the ship, he raced along the dock, leaping over crates, dodging carts and barrels. He scanned his surroundings as he ran. Surely there was something that could help him gain access to the ship—some way he might still be able to get aboard.

From the deck of the *Purgatory*, Willa and Porter were shouting, and jumping up and down to get his attention.

Their words slowly penetrated the fog of panic that surrounded him.

"The gates! The gates!"

Breathing hard, Tom drew to a stop. The towering walled gates of Divino loomed just ahead. He peered through the night and realized why Porter and Willa had been so frantic. The enormous, impenetrable gates—gates toward which the *Purgatory* coasted at an impressive clip—were firmly bolted shut. The gatekeepers who monitored the river traffic had either been taken by scavengers or had deserted their post. Either way, the *Purgatory* was headed for disaster.

Umbrey's ship was sturdy, but it was no match for massive wooden gates reinforced with thick bands of iron. A collision would almost certainly shatter the hull, splintering the ship into pieces.

While half of Umbrey's crew was occupied battling the scavengers who had slunk aboard, the other half loosened the rigging to let the sails go limp in an attempt to slow the vessel. It worked, but only to a degree. The tide, which they'd raced to catch, propelled them relentlessly toward the gates.

Until that moment, Tom had merely been keeping pace with the ship. Now he sprinted faster.

The guard tower was tall and rectangular, with an interior staircase that twisted upward at least one hundred feet off the ground. Tightening his grip on his torch, he threw open the door and bounded up the stairs, terrified that with each twist of the staircase he'd come face-to-face with a scavenger.

Incredibly, his luck held. He reached the top, breathing hard. The guardroom was empty. No sign of scavengers. Tom's gaze flew to the thick wooden lever in the center of the floor. He slipped his torch in an empty sconce and threw himself upon the release. He heaved and tugged, but the lever wouldn't budge.

He repositioned himself and tried again, his jaw clenched and his muscles trembled as he strained to shove it forward. Finally he felt a slight give, and the iron bar, which opened via a series of interlocking cogs and levers, groaned upward.

The gates parted ever so slightly, like a massive door cracking ajar. A further series of ropes and pulleys were necessary to draw the wooden barriers fully open, but he simply didn't have time to operate them. The *Purgatory* might hit the gates, but at least the vessel would make it through. That would have to do.

As Tom peered out a narrow window in the guard tower, the shape of an idea took hold—a plan that might just get him back aboard. Moving solely on instinct, he slipped through the small opening and stepped out onto the topmost edge of the wooden gate. The beam was twelve inches across, easily wide enough to accommodate him. As the gate wasn't secured, it swayed as he lowered himself atop it, but only a little.

Holding out his arms for balance, he crouched down low and carefully crept toward the opening where the two panels met. He reached the end of the gate and fixed his gaze on the *Purgatory's* approach. The *Purgatory* sailed straight toward him. Perfect. Now all he had to do was get a little closer . . .

The ship was nearly there, sailing straight toward him. He had a clear shot to the main mast. He took a deep breath and readied himself. From his vantage point atop the gate, he would be nearly eye-to-eye with the crow's nest. All he had to do was reach out, grab it, and then climb down the rigging until he reached the deck.

His plan was simple. Almost foolproof. And if he hadn't misjudged the breadth of the *Purgatory's* hull, it might have worked.

Instead, the ship's starboard side slammed into the gate as it passed, knocking him off the top of the gate as if shaking a monkey from a tree.

Tom managed to throw out his arms and kick off the beam as he fell, thrusting himself toward the ship's foremost mast. His fingers brushed rope, but closed on air. Rough canvas grazed

his cheek. He twisted and turned, but couldn't catch hold of anything to slow his descent. He tumbled wildly, careening headfirst down one of the *Purgatory's* sails as though he was riding an enormous canvas slide.

He finally managed to grab a rope as his shoulder hit the edge of a horizontal mast that divided the upper and lower. He caught it with both hands and held on tight. He swung out wide, sailing over the river and back across the deck, knocking down two of Umbrey's men in the process—both of whom had been too busy fighting scavengers to pay attention to Tom's wild acrobatics.

His second pass over the deck wasn't quite as dramatic. Unable to direct his flight, he slammed straight into the mainmast, hitting it dead-on. The force of the impact sent him reeling backwards. Once again he found himself lying flat on his back, blinking up at the night sky. The ship pitched and rolled beneath him as he fought to regain his senses.

For the second time that evening, Umbrey leaned over him, his scruffy face blocking the night sky.

"You know, lad, there are easier ways to come aboard."

Beside him, Porter let out a sharp breath. "Oh, but we couldn't have that. Then he might not be the center of attention."

Tom looked at his brother. Ignoring the protests of his aching ribs—he'd slammed the mast *hard*—he eased himself into a sitting position. "What?"

"You heard me."

Porter stood with his arms crossed over his chest, his features tightened in an expression of simmering hostility. As though he actually believed Tom had *wanted* to tumble off the gate, slide headfirst through the rigging, crash into the main mast, and risk splitting his skull like an overripe melon. Just to get a little attention.

Willa stepped between them. "Look, forget it, both of you. We all made it aboard and that's what matters. We can't fight among ourselves. Not if we want to get the book." Turning to Tom, she said, "Now, are you all right?"

He rose and stepped around her, standing nearly toe-to-toe with his brother. "What's your problem?"

"No problem." Porter gave a cool shrug. "It's been a while. I guess I'd just forgotten how you love to play the hero."

"*Play the hero?* Are you serious?"

"We had a plan. All you had to do was get on the ship. But I guess that was a little too complicated for you."

"What'd you expect me to do? Just stand there and let those scavengers attack that woman and her kids?"

"It wasn't about you! Her husband was right there, seconds away. But you had to go and risk everything—"

"And what if I hadn't?" Tom challenged. "What if I'd just followed you aboard? You would have crashed into those gates. That's what would have happened. This ship would be torn to pieces, and we'd all be in that river right now, fighting off scavengers. Think about it. Is that what you want?"

Porter's eyes went icy. "Like I said, you're a hero. You saved us all."

A sharp gust of wind blew across the deck. The upper sail, likely the one he became tangled up in when he'd fallen, bellowed out with a deafening *crack!* Tom's rope whipped past them, slithering across the deck like some kind of underwater snake.

"Where's my crew?!" Umbrey bellowed. "Do you lazy bilge rats need to be told to tighten the halyard line?!"

A sailor sprung to and secured the wayward line. Umbrey watched the man see to his task, then returned his attention to Porter, Willa, Mudge, and Tom.

"I've got bigger problems on my hands than your petty little squabbles. I run a ship here, not a blasted nursery. Split up and cool off." He looked at Willa and Mudge. "You two go below decks and get some sleep. And you two . . . " He reached for a pair of long wooden poles equipped with vicious-looking iron hooks. He thrust one pole into Tom's hands, the other in Porter's. "You start on the starboard side, you start on the port. Comb the hull for scavengers. You find any of those slimy creatures, hook 'em and cast them far enough out to sea that they can't come back. You let one sneak onto my ship and I'll personally feed you to it. Understood?"

Tom gave a tight nod, as did Porter.

"Good. Get to it."

Willa sent them both a fuming glare and stormed away without a word, which made Tom feel far worse than Umbrey's scolding had. She was right. If they were going to make it through the Cursed Souls Sea, he would have to find a way to get along with his brother.

By the time he had finished his task (he'd only found one scavenger on his side, but judging by the hissing and howling and subsequent splashes he'd heard on the opposite side of the ship, Porter had had to deal with three), he was considerably calmer. He triple-checked to make sure he hadn't missed any, then returned his pole to its proper place by the main mast.

He looked around. Porter was gone. The flickering lights and shrill chaos of Divino were long gone. Umbrey's crew, or at least the ones who remained above deck, moved about their tasks with quiet efficiency. The stars had shifted. Time had passed, but there was no way to guess how much. An inky black sea surrounded them. It lapped against the hull, setting a soft, steady rhythm to the night.

Tom was suddenly aware how exhausted he was. His muscles ached and his eyes were sore with the strain of keeping them open. He wanted to find Umbrey and find out more about the scavengers, but his thoughts were too cloudy. Better to wait until the morning.

He'd followed a crewman below decks earlier that night when he'd changed his clothes. Not knowing where else to go, he headed in the same general direction, hoping he'd stumble upon the sleeping quarters. The *Purgatory* was a large ship, fitted with rough-hewn ladders that led from one level to the next. Tom wandered through a maze of dimly lit passageways, descending deeper and deeper into the belly of the ship.

The thick scent of kerosene oil and greased gears greeted him as he moved lower, causing him to wonder if Umbrey used some sort of engine to power his ship, a mechanical thrust to give them extra power beyond the capacity of the sails. But he quickly dropped the thought as he came upon the crew's quarters.

It was a large, low room with maybe thirty hammocks suspended from the ceiling joists. A chorus of deep, throaty snores greeted him as he entered. A single lantern, the wick turned down low, hung from a central beam and gave the room a shadowy glow.

He spied Porter, his pale blond head a beacon in the darkness, sitting in a hammock at the far edge of the room. A lone empty hammock swung beside him. Tom bit back a sigh and warily approached him. He'd hoped, after their argument, to put a little distance between them, but apparently that wasn't going to happen.

"Where are Willa and Mudge?" he asked.

Porter tilted his chin toward a blanket that had been hung in the corner, providing Willa a makeshift space for privacy. Mudge rocked in a hammock on the opposite side of the blanket, fast asleep.

Tom turned back to find him holding two pewter mugs brimming with a warm, sweet-smelling liquid. He passed one to Tom.

"Here."

The unexpected gesture surprised him. He regarded Porter curiously. Was the offer of a drink an apology for lashing out at him or a sign he meant to start over? Or neither one? The only thing Tom was sure of was that his brother looked as exhausted as he felt.

He lifted the mug but hesitated at the unfamiliar smell. Grog? he wondered. He wasn't exactly sure what that was, but he'd heard pirates drank it aboard ship. All he knew was that at the academy, being caught with anything alcoholic resulted in an automatic suspension, and he was pretty sure Lost would apply that rule to the Five Kingdoms as well. Still, the drink smelled delicious.

"What is it?"

"*Slipper*. Sugared milk and spices, mostly." He shrugged. "The cook sent it down from the galley."

Tom took a cautious sip.

Rich and foamy, the drink bubbled slightly as though carbonated. It was warm and soothing at the same time, with a sweet caramel aftertaste.

"It's good."

Porter nodded. "Our mother used to make it for me when I was a boy and couldn't sleep." He drew up one knee and rested his arm atop it. A faraway expression softened his features, as though he was caught up in some warm, distant memory.

Tom fought back envy. Porter had enjoyed a lifetime with

their parents. He had memory after memory to draw upon. Tom had nothing. Just a portrait given to him months ago with their likenesses. But those images were flat, with no voice or flesh to them at all. Impossible to picture what sort of people his parents had been. Sort of like trying to imagine an entire dinosaur when all he'd been given was a prehistoric pinky toe.

He glanced at Porter, watching as he sipped his foamy brew, and allowed his mind to wander. What if they'd been raised together, as brothers? Would there still be the same simmering tension between them? Or would they maybe, just maybe, get along? Would they have spent nights sipping—Tom searched his mind for the word—*slipper* together, staying up late to build forts, tell stories, and all the other stuff brothers did when they were growing up? Would that have changed anything?

Porter's thoughts must have been running in a similar vein, for he gestured to his mug and asked, "Do you have something like this in your world?"

Tom took another sip. It was more than good. It was warm and sweet and strangely comforting. He nodded. "Hot chocolate."

Porter's pale brows knit together. "Does it taste like this?"

"No. It's . . . " He searched his mind, groping for a way to describe the taste of hot chocolate to someone who'd never tried it before. "It's sweet and smooth, but kind of darker, with more of an edge to it. And sometimes there are marshmallows on top."

His words made no sense, but he couldn't come up with any better way to describe the drink. Porter nodded politely and looked away, his expression once again carefully guarded. In that instant, Tom understood they'd both reached the same conclusion. Trying to connect after so many years was futile. The gulf between them was simply too wide.

Porter set down his mug. "You get 'em all?"

"Yeah." Tom visualized the scavenger he'd scraped off into sea. An ugly, hideous thing with sunken gray skin, tangled tufts of hair protruding from its skull, and jagged yellow teeth. He couldn't tell if it had been male or female.

"There aren't any scavengers in your world?" Porter asked.

"No."

Tom thought about mentioning the zombies he'd seen in horror films, but everybody knew those weren't *real*. Not like here. And scavenger hunts? A silly party game where teams ran door-to-door looking for things like tiny paper umbrellas, a pair of dice, or a purple shoelace. Random things like that.

Once again he was struck by how parallel their worlds seemed, only his had been put through a filter of safety, with all the ugliness and danger rubbed away.

Porter stretched back in his hammock, his hands tucked behind his head, staring up at the low ceiling. "Earlier tonight— you don't have to be like that, you know."

"Like what?"

"Like it's all up to you to be the hero. Rushing in like you're the only one who can save us."

"That's not what I did."

His brother let out a sharp breath that indicated, better than any words could have, he didn't agree. Thick silence hung between them. Porter was the first to break it.

"It's too late, anyway. You wasted your time coming here. We've already lost. No map can change that—especially not a cursed one."

Tom looked at him. "What happened? How did everything get so bad?"

"It just . . . did."

"And the scavengers? What are they? Where did they come from?"

Porter continued to stare at the ceiling. Though he didn't say a word, his expression changed, becoming harder, more closed off than usual. He rolled over, presenting his back to Tom.

"It's late," he said. "You can ask your questions in the morning."

Tom noted that he didn't say he would answer them, only that he could ask them. A minor distinction, but an important one.

A few moments later he heard Porter's breath change, and knew from the rise and fall of his shoulders he had fallen asleep. Tom wasn't sure he'd be able to sleep at all. He was exhausted physically, but his thoughts were racing. As he set down his mug and stretched out in his hammock, his fingers brushed the folly's rattle he'd stuffed in his pocket. Incredibly, he'd forgotten all about it.

He drew it out and held it up, admiring its pinkish-orange glow. It was hot, but not burning, just warm enough to fill his hand with dry heat. He watched it throb in a steady rhythm, somehow matching the cycle of his pulse, beat for beat. Almost as though it was directly connected to his heart.

A wish, he thought. He could wish for anything . . .

He blinked heavily. The combined effects of the warm drink and softly swaying hammock were rocking him to sleep. He tucked the rattle away and pulled up the rough wool blanket folded at his feet.

Porter was wrong. It wasn't over yet. Tomorrow, he thought, as he closed his eyes. He'd figure everything out tomorrow.

CHAPTER EIGHT

A shrill bell pierced the silence. Tom clenched his teeth in irritation and attempted without success to block out the noise.

Just two more minutes, he thought, burrowing deeper into his bed. He shrugged his blanket over his shoulder and rolled over, only to suddenly realize two strange things: his bed was swaying, and coarse rope rubbed his cheek where his pillow should have been.

For a moment, he could make no sense of where he was. Then it hit him. He wasn't in his dorm room at the academy anymore, but on Umbrey's ship, the *Purgatory*. His eyes flew open and he sat up, shaking off the foggy cloud of sleep that held him in its grip. Next to him, Porter's hammock was empty.

He glanced around the room. The other hammocks were full, but the occupants looked different from the shadowy glimpses he'd had of the men who'd been sleeping last night. A crew shift, he guessed.

He slipped out of his hammock and hunted around until he found the bathroom. The space consisted of a small stool and rough table with soap, a water pitcher, and wash basin. He understood how those items might be used to clean himself, but he didn't understand why that was all there was to the room. He looked around blankly. For a desperate moment, he considered waking one of Umbrey's crewmen to ask him where the toilet was, but the idea was too mortifying to seriously entertain.

The words *The Necessary*, scrawled across a hatched portal in the floor, caught his attention. He cautiously eased open the door and found himself staring, through a small opening perhaps ten inches beneath him, at the ocean. No plumbing or drains to worry about here. Evidently everything was immediately flushed out to sea. Now *that* was definitely something he hadn't read about in any history book.

He finished and soaped up, splashed water on his face, rinsed his mouth, and tugged his fingers through his hair. Once the basics had been taken care of, he realized how hungry he was. He climbed up to the main deck. A mild sun shone directly overhead, making it near noon, he noted with surprise. He couldn't recall the last time he'd slept so late. No wonder he was famished.

Umbrey spied him and waved him over. "'Bout time you got out of bed. I was beginning to think you'd tumbled overboard."

As there was no reply he could possibly make, Tom ignored the comment, choosing instead to say hello to Willa, Mudge, and Porter, who stood beside Umbrey on the quarterdeck. Their greetings were friendly enough, but Tom couldn't help noticing the quiet tension that ran through the group.

He turned his attention to the surrounding sea. A shroud of heavy mist rose from the surface of the water, giving it a sinister, swamp-like appearance. The horizon was dotted with a series of small, rocky islands, through which the *Purgatory* carefully navigated. Free-floating masses of algae, some of them thick enough to support a man, drifted past. Tom had been in a decent mood when he woke up, but no longer. The creepiness of the place sent a wave of dread through him.

"Is this the Cursed Souls Sea?" he asked.

Umbrey shook his head. "The Straits of Dire." He rapped a knuckle on the map mounted beside the ship's wheel. "We're here, between northeastern end of Aquat and the Cursed Souls

Sea. If we make it through, we'll continue on."

If, Tom noted, not when.

Willa rubbed her hands over her arms, as though warding off a chill. "We're passing through the trade route," she said.

The trade route. Tom mulled over her words, thinking of the vast cargoes of goods that left Asia aboard enormous ships bound for Europe. "You mean, like spices and silks?"

Porter, who'd been scanning the horizon as well, gave a barely imperceptible shake of his head. "Slaves," he said. "Aquat slavers claim these waters. There's a penalty for traversing them."

"What sort of penalty?"

"One I'm not willing to pay," Umbrey answered flatly. He lifted a spyglass to his eye and slowly surveyed the horizon. A long, narrow island jutted out of the sea directly ahead of them, slicing the channel in two. Umbrey lowered his spy glass and glanced from Tom to Porter. "Well, mapmaker's sons? Which is it? The northern route or the southern one?"

"North," said Porter.

"South," said Tom.

"Naturally," said Umbrey, a wry smile curving his lips. He arched a shaggy brow and looked at Mudge. "Well, majesty? It appears a royal verdict is needed."

Mudge smiled. "We'll go south. Tom's way."

Tom mussed Mudge's hair. "Excellent choice." Although he

kept his tone light, he didn't miss the way Porter stiffened.

Umbrey conveyed the order to his crew and the *Purgatory* veered to starboard, entering the channel through the southern side. That accomplished, he nodded to a crewman standing just over Tom's shoulder.

"The cannon ready?"

"Aye."

"Good." Umbrey nodded. "Tell the men to keep to their stations until we leave these waters."

Tom glanced across the deck. Compared to the frantic pace of the night before, the ship was relatively calm. But he noticed something he hadn't seen before. Umbrey's men were battle-ready. Cannons had been 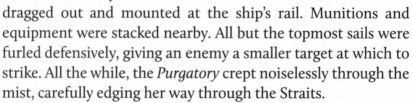 dragged out and mounted at the ship's rail. Munitions and equipment were stacked nearby. All but the topmost sails were furled defensively, giving an enemy a smaller target at which to strike. All the while, the *Purgatory* crept noiselessly through the mist, carefully edging her way through the Straits.

"What about the scavengers?" Tom asked. "Where—"

"Later, lad," Umbrey said, cutting him off. He passed his spyglass to a crewman. "Keep a tight watch. If you spot so much as a castaway on a coconut raft, feel free to blast him out of the water."

"Aye, Cap'n."

Umbrey motioned for them to follow him as he left the quarterdeck, muttering to himself as he walked, "Never could stand these waters. Bad feel to 'em. The sooner we get out of here, the better."

He led them to a cabin below decks, just off the ship's galley. An enormous desk, piled high with a messy assortment of papers and maps, took up the rear wall. In the center of the room a weathered pine table stood. Five place settings rested atop it. To the left of the table was a sideboard loaded with food.

Rich, delectable aromas wafted around Tom, putting a note of urgency to his hunger. He needed to eat *now*.

"Food first," Umbrey said as he ushered them inside. "Then we talk."

Tom let Willa and Mudge precede him, but he didn't mind edging in front of Porter. They each grabbed a plate, loading up on different kinds of fish (which Tom had expected), as well as salads brimming with fruits and nuts, roasted vegetables, mashed potatoes and gravy, dark loaves of bread, and pastas tossed with creamy sauces (which he hadn't expected at all).

"I don't believe in serving gruel," Umbrey announced as they ate. "Something about the sea stirs a man's appetite. Besides which, men fight better on a full belly. How can you ask your crew to keep a proper watch when all they're thinking about are their stomachs?"

Umbrey took a deep swig from his mug and let out a satisfied belch. He looked better than Tom had ever seen him. His crew might be a rough lot, but if anyone ever invented a Best Dressed Pirate award, Umbrey would win it hands down. He wore a cream-colored silk shirt with a ruffled front, a deep plum velvet coat, and emerald green knee breeches. He'd even polished his peg leg. It gleamed with a rich mahogany sheen. His manners however, needed a little work, Tom thought, watching as Umbrey dragged the lace cuff of his shirt through the gravy.

Tom finished his second helping of mashed potatoes and said, "Keegan said something about Salamaine's curse. What was he talking about?"

The mood around the table, which hadn't exactly been light, darkened. Porter's jaw tightened. Willa pushed her plate away.

Umbrey speared a chunk of fried octopus. He popped it in his mouth and chewed slowly, his expression somber. "It's a dark story. But I suppose it all begins with that sword..."

A heavy silence fell across the table as their gazes were drawn to the Sword of Five Kingdoms, which rested on the table between Mudge and Willa.

"What do you mean?" Tom asked.

Willa bent her head and drew her fingers over the sword's golden grip, lightly tracing the five glittering black stones embedded there. In a low voice, as though making a confession, she said, "You saw it, with the scavengers at the courthouse. It won't work anymore."

Tom's back went cold. He'd seen that, but he hadn't really thought about it. He suddenly understood why they'd all appeared so defeated. Why Porter had said he was too late, they'd already lost. "But . . . it can't just *break*."

His brother looked at him. "You remember the sword was a gift from Marrick, a wizard who believed in the good of mankind."

"Yeah. So?"

"There were those who objected to Marrick's gift from the very beginning," Willa said. "Those who thought men should never be able to hold such power in their grasp. That we weren't capable of decency, justice, honor. Pernicus was such a wizard. He had no faith in mankind."

"But Salamaine *was* good. That was the whole point. Marrick found someone who proved that good could win over evil."

Umbrey sighed and leaned back in his chair. "Aye. Salamaine was good. And kind and brave and just. But he was also a man. Think on it, lad. Are there some men who are wholly good, while others are wholly bad? Or does the line between good and evil run through each of our hearts—a line so fine we risk crossing it at any moment, with every decision we make and every action we take?"

Tom hesitated, not sure how to answer. A rap sounded on the door. Two crewmen entered and cleared the table and sideboard. They left, closing the door behind them.

"You should know all of it," Willa said. She went quiet for a moment, gathering her thoughts. Willa had a slight build, and at first glance gave the impression of being delicate, almost frail. But she was tougher—and braver—than most guys Tom had ever met.

"Salamaine's rule was one of peace and prosperity," she began. "Greater peace and prosperity than the world had ever known. But a score of years into his reign the prophets came to him with dark visions. Warnings of death and despair. They foretold a violent struggle for his throne, resulting in the utter destruction of everything he'd worked for."

Porter nodded. "They told him the Five Kingdoms would be divided in war for centuries to come unless he did something to stop it."

"What was he supposed to stop?" Tom asked, still not following.

"The prophets told him that a dark-haired boy, aged sixteen years, was plotting against him," Willa answered. "That this boy would soon pull together a legion of his own and lead an uprising against him. They told him that the boy was already scheming, that it was written in the stars, that he had to act *now*, at once, or he would be too late. He would lose everything."

"You can imagine how painful it was for Salamaine to hear this," Umbrey said. "He had a kingdom to protect, a wife he loved, and two fine boys barely out of the cradle." He paused, sending Tom a look of quiet significance. "You'll recall, of course, that Salamaine had two sons."

"Twins," Porter reminded him. "One light and pure hearted"—he inclined his head, gesturing to himself, then he motioned toward Tom—"the other one brash and greedy, utterly dark in body, mind, and spirit."

Tom didn't miss the jibe, nor was Porter's meaning lost on him. He knew, of course, how Salamaine's tale ended: in a vicious play for power, his own son rose up against him, destroying everything Salamaine had spent a lifetime building and pitching the Five Kingdoms into centuries of brutal chaos.

"The problem was," Willa continued, "the prophets were wrong. Or rather, they misinterpreted the signs. The threat wasn't from a sixteen-year-old, dark-haired boy, but a dark-haired boy sixteen years *hence*."

Umbrey sighed. "Of course, there was no way for Salamaine to know that."

"So what did he do?" Tom asked.

"At first, he ignored it," answered Porter. "Hoping it would all go away, I suppose. That was a mistake. Whispers and warnings spread throughout the kingdom as the prophecies grew increasingly dire. Citizens took up arms on their own. Mobs roamed the streets at night, hunting for dark-haired boys. Neighbor turned against neighbor. People were frightened to leave their homes."

"Salamaine knew he had to do something," Umbrey said, "so he devised a plan—a clever plan, by my view. You see, at this time he'd received word of newly discovered riches. Thick veins of gold had been unearthed in the remote islands north of Aquat. Rather than arrest and imprison all dark-haired boys of sixteen, he ordered them to sail to these islands and work the mines."

"It was a banishment of sorts, but a generous one," Willa interjected. "They would be allowed to keep a portion of the gold they mined, thus securing their futures. In ten years time, it was agreed they would be allowed to return to the Five Kingdoms, if they so chose."

"Not everyone agreed with Salamaine's solution," Porter said. "His closest advisors thought he was too lenient."

"Lenient? Ten years forced labor?" Tom interjected. "That sounds harsh to me."

"Maybe for some." Porter shrugged. "Others came from homes where it was a struggle to put food on the table. For them, this was an opportunity."

"Even so, there were misgivings to the plan," Willa said. "Doubts as to whether Salamaine had truly solved the problem, or just put it off for a decade or so."

Tom took that in.

"In any event, it was done." Umbrey drank deeply from his pewter tankard, then set it down with a solid *thunk*. A foamy mustache remained on his upper lip. He wiped it off with his sleeve. "On the first of May, amidst much celebration, the boys, along with any of their families or friends who chose to accompany them, were packed aboard the *Mayday* and shipped off. It was a lively event. A new beginning, a new venture, new riches. As far as most were concerned, the crisis was solved."

"So it was over?" Tom asked.

"No." Willa looked at Tom. "Salamaine followed aboard the *Justice*, his royal vessel. His goal was to see the boys off—make certain they were well and truly removed from his kingdom."

"It might have worked," Porter interrupted. "But they ran into troubled seas. On the third day out, a rogue wave struck the *Mayday*, capsizing the vessel."

Silence.

Umbrey sighed. "The sinking occurred not far from here where the currents are most treacherous. To this day, the cry of *Mayday! Mayday!* can mean only one thing: a ship in dire distress."

He took another deep swig and shook his head. "It must have been a pitiful sight. Boys not much older than you and Porter, others as young as Mudge. Parents, grandparents, sisters, all of them flailing about in the water, crying out for help. And what nasty water it was. Icy cold, full of follies, sharks, squid, and other assorted hungry beasties. They had no chance."

"No chance?" Tom countered. "Wasn't the *Justice* sailing right behind them?"

Porter shot him a hard look. "Haven't you been listening?"

"Yes, but—"

"Salamaine ordered his crew to stand down," Willa said softly. "As the *Mayday* sank, Salamaine stood by and watched them all drown."

CHAPTER NINE

A BITTER LEGACY

A hollow feeling spread through Tom's chest, as though the air had been slowly sucked from his lungs.

"He watched them all drown? His own people?"

"Aye, lad. He did."

Tom shook his head, staring at them all as though they'd gone crazy. "Wait a minute. Wait a minute. I thought Salamaine was the *good* guy. The hero. That was the whole point of *everything.*"

"Nothing's ever that simple, lad."

"Tom," Willa said, "if you'll just listen—"

"To what? More of your stories?" Righteous anger heated Tom's blood. He felt tricked, duped into believing something that had been a total lie. He glared at her. "You're the one who told me about that sword. You said that its power would only be awakened in the hands of someone pure, just, and good. Someone like Salamaine, or Mudge. I believed you."

"Because it's true."

"True?" Tom gave an ugly laugh. "Then explain to me why he allowed everyone to die like that." An image of Keegan chained to the wall of his jail cell flashed into his mind. "Keegan was right. Salamaine was no better than he is."

Like a spark hitting dry tinder, his words fanned a flame. Willa, Porter, and Umbrey all erupted in fiery denials, shouting at Tom—and each other—across the table. But it was Mudge who drew everyone's attention.

He stood, lifted the Sword of Five Kingdoms, and drove it into the center of the table. The blade dug into the soft pine and stayed there, the hilt reverberating with the force of the strike.

Mudge stared at them. "He did it because he felt he had no other choice."

For a moment, Tom was too shocked to speak. He simply looked at Mudge. In that instant, he realized he hadn't really *seen* Mudge since his return to the Five Kingdoms. Oh, he'd taken Porter's measure, smirked at Umbrey's taste for pirate frippery, felt weirdly self-conscious when Willa (who really was far prettier than he'd remembered) had hugged him. But Mudge had just been Mudge—the scrawny, scruffy-haired boy who tagged along on their adventure.

Perhaps that had once been true, but it wasn't the case any longer. Just as one might look at a puppy's paws and predict the size of the adult dog, the same was true of Mudge. In that moment, Tom had a glimpse of the man—the *ruler*—the boy might one day become. He had a presence about him now, a weight in his stare and a gravity to his bearing that seemed oddly appropriate, despite his age. Until that moment, Mudge had been content to listen to the others tell Salamaine's story. But no longer.

"He did it because he felt he had no other choice," he repeated. "The fate of the Five Kingdoms rested on his actions, and his alone." He looked at Tom. "Imagine it. Imagine for a moment if the lives of thousands were hinged on *you*. On every word you uttered, every choice you made, every action you took, every day for as long as you lived. Imagine you were there, with the screaming and the shouting and the boat sinking, and just a split second to decide what to do."

Tom hesitated. He wanted to rail against Salamaine, to insist he wasn't capable of something that horrific, that he would never make a mistake like that—because everything he did was well thought out and perfectly planned. Except, of course, it wasn't.

"I can't imagine it."

"Then *listen*, lad, for there's more to the tale."

Mudge tilted his chin toward Porter. "Go on, then."

"Salamaine was hailed as the harbinger of light," Porter said. "He was . . . " he hesitated for a moment, as though searching for the right word, "*revered*. He was Marrick's chosen. People looked to him for more than just food and shelter. They wanted justice, peace, and protection. Not just for them, but for their children, and their children's children."

"That's why the prophecy was so terrible," Willa continued. "If Salamaine didn't answer the challenge directly, he risked destroying everything for generations to come. He must have worried whether he was doing all he could to protect his kingdoms, whether he should have been doing more. So when the wave hit the *Mayday* . . . " she paused, lifting her shoulders in a helpless shrug.

"It must have appeared to be the perfect solution to his problem," Porter said. "A gift from the fates. Every dark-haired, sixteen-year-old boy gone. The threat neatly resolved. He didn't have to kill them, or imprison them, or send them away and worry what might happen when they returned in ten years time. All he had to do was *not* save them."

Mudge nodded grimly. "The death of a few innocents, in exchange for the lives of many thousands."

Silence, thick and heavy, descended upon the room.

Mudge reached for the Sword of Five Kingdoms and plucked it from the center of the table. "Keegan called it a cursed sword. He was wrong." He tilted it slightly and held it up for Tom to see. "On one side, Marrick's blade. Every good action Salamaine took magnified a thousandfold. But on the other side . . . the blade of Pernicus. Every evil action Salamaine took magnified a thousandfold, as well."

"Two powerful blades forged together into one sword," Willa said. "A symbol of the good and evil that cuts through all of us."

"So that's Salamaine's curse?" Tom asked.

Porter gave a curt shake of his head. "The scavengers are Salamaine's curse. You see, all those aboard the *Mayday* perished, but they didn't die. For centuries, the Cursed Souls Sea has kept them alive. Or at least, undead. It's meant to serve as a reminder of the evil that lurks within all of us."

Tom shuddered. He could still smell their stench. Mudge tapped the edge of the blade against the table. "Since Salamaine created the scavengers, this blade is powerless to stop them. With every day that passes, the scavengers become stronger, and this sword becomes weaker."

"So what do we do?" asked Tom.

"The Black Book of Pernicus," Porter said. "His magic created the scavengers. It's said his book holds the answer to finally ridding the Five Kingdoms of them." He reached for the map of the Cursed Souls Sea and spread it across the table.

Looking at it, Willa shivered and rubbed her upper arms. "My grandfather used to say only a fool would enter the Cursed Souls Sea."

Umbrey grunted. "Aye, but we're the fools with the map to do it." He pushed up the dainty sleeves of his shirt (displaying hairy, muscular biceps that Tom thought were far better left covered, even if he was wearing a shirt that looked like the upper half of a wedding gown) and leaned against the edge of the table. "Well?" he demanded, glaring at Tom and Porter. "What in blazes are you waiting for? This isn't a pleasure cruise. The Black Book of Pernicus. Where do we find it?"

Keegan stood at the edge of a rocky promontory overlooking the Cursed Souls Sea. Sharp gusts of wind tugged at his cape, causing it to billow about his shoulders like a swirling black cloud. He placed one booted foot atop a low boulder and leaned forward, peering into the distance.

Umbrey's ship had departed hours ago and wouldn't return for days hence, yet he could feel his impatience brewing inside him, churning and writhing like the sea itself. The Black Book of Pernicus. It was just a matter of time until it was his. All he had to do was wait—a task for which his temperament was supremely unsuited.

He cut a bored glance at his surroundings. His army, The Watch, was spread out in the surrounding woods keeping guard. Their torches flickered even in the light of day. The precaution was unnecessary. There were no signs of the scavengers here. Not yet, at least. Unlike Divino, which sat at the heart of the Five Kingdoms, the coastal regions had yet to be overrun.

Behind Keegan was the sprawling, seaside town of Blinding Beacon Falls. As he turned his gaze to the jumbled rocks at the base of the cliff, a beacon of light stung his eyes. The beacon was meant to be friendly, but Keegan had taken up residence and would use it for his own evil end.

On moonless nights he would use the beacon to lure unsuspecting ships toward the rocky shoals. The captains of those ships believed themselves in safe harbor until the mirrors within the lighthouse were flipped around. The light intensified, blinding the crew, and causing the ship to run aground. It had been easy to raid the ship, steal the cargo, and engage the crew in a murderous brawl. The good people there were fleeing as far inland as they could go.

Coarse laughter sounded in the tavern behind him. The tavern door opened and the proprietor stepped out, overseeing four men who carried a small oak table and a pair of chairs. Once the proprietor showed his men where to place the table, he withdrew a dishcloth, brushed off the table's surface, and swept the chairs clean.

With a nervous flourish of his hands, he gestured for Keegan to sit. "This is an unexpected honor, sire," he said. "Can I offer you something to drink? Something to eat? A bottle of my finest wine?"

Keegan remained standing. He arched a single dark brow and frowned at the man. "Are you suggesting the wine served in your hovel would be fit for me?"

Beads of sweat sprouted along the man's forehead. "No, no, of course not," he stammered. "Forgive me, sire. Perhaps, then, a jug of cool water—"

"A jug of water? For whom? Me, or my horse?"

"I . . . that is . . . " The proprietor gazed about in desperation, as though looking for a hole he could sink into.

"Leave me."

"Yes, sire." He walked, almost ran, back inside the tavern.

When Keegan turned again, he found he was no longer alone. A dark-haired woman appeared an arms length away, quietly watching him. *Shimmering* and ghostlike, she hung just out of reach, nearly swallowed by the shadows. It was as though she wasn't really there at all, and might disappear as quickly as she had appeared.

Accompanying her, perched on the back of one of the chairs the proprietor's men had brought out, was a large, stately bird with brilliant red plumage.

"Vivienne," Keegan said by way of a greeting. He gave a low, courtly bow, then pressed a kiss against the back of her hand. Her skin felt like ice to the touch.

"You're late."

Ignoring him, Vivienne moved toward the cliff edge. The fabric of her gown, rich blues and greens, swirled around her ankles like a living stream. She studied the sea for a long moment, then lifted her gaze to Keegan's. Her eyes were as hard and cool as emeralds.

"You gave them my map?"

"Yes."

"Excellent." She turned back to the sea. "They're out there now, aren't they? They've gone after the black book. I can feel it." A small, cruel smile curved her lips. "Is it true that scavengers overrun the city?"

"Yes."

"Ah." It was not so much an acknowledgement, as a purr of satisfaction. "So I was right. The magic of Pernicus remains strong."

Keegan eyed her curiously. "If you wanted the black book, you could have given the dark map directly to the mapmaker's sons. Yet you brought both the map and the key to me."

She gave a cool nod. "Yes. I did."

"Why?"

"Does it matter?"

"It shouldn't. But I find I have a curious nature."

"Very well." Vivienne trailed her hands along the length of her skirts. As she moved, Keegan heard a subtle sound, a vibration that fell somewhere between the tinkling of ice and the chiming of high-pitched bells.

"Black Book of Pernicus," she said. "They will bring it to you. But Umbrey, the one-legged one, he knows too much. He studied too long at the elbow of the Hero Twin's father. He would never willingly allow the book to fall into my hands. Neither would Marrick's chosen, that boy king." She turned, facing him directly. "You, however, you are reasonable. We understand one another."

"Yes. We do." Keegan's gaze narrowed. "As long as I get what I want from the bargain."

"Of course. Control of your little kingdoms. You shall have it."

"And you? What will you get?"

Icy brilliance shimmered in her eyes. "Everything else."

The statement hung in the air between them for a long moment, then she moved toward the chair. "Now that all is in place, I will ensure that nothing goes wrong." She stroked the crimson bird, then lifted her arm and pointed toward the sky, giving an order in a language Keegan had never before heard.

The bird lifted its enormous wings, pumped them once against the air, and soared off into the sky. Keegan followed its path over the Cursed Souls Sea.

When he turned back, Vivienne was gone. The only sign she'd been there at all was a single crimson feather, which drifted from the sky and landed on the ground beside his boot.

CHAPTER TEN

FLAG

OF

SACRIFICE

The *Purgatory* continued its steady passage, the helmsman steering cautiously through the Straits of Dire. Within the galley cabin, Tom took up a position at one end of the rough pine table, while Porter stationed himself at the opposite end. The island of Arx had shown itself earlier, giving them a general idea of the direction in which they needed to travel, but now they needed specifics. Exactly how were they supposed to get there?

At Porter's nod, they brought their fingertips to rest on the edges of the map. The instant Tom touched the parchment, a sharp tingle rushed up his forearms, shooting past his elbows and zinging across his shoulder blades.

He'd once seen a cat nibble on a live extension cord. Although he could never know exactly how the cat had felt as the electric current had zipped through its nerves—he had only seen the startled feline arch its back, hiss, and run away—Tom had a strong suspicion that the unpleasant sensation he'd just experienced was exactly the same.

At least this time he didn't feel seasick. The pitch and gentle rolling of the *Purgatory* helped counter that effect. He watched as the sea depicted on the map sprang to life, waves crashing against each other in a whirling, writhing mass of cross currents, riptides, water spouts, and treacherous ocean swells. Just below the turbulent surface of the water Tom caught glimpses of slithering nests of follies, their serpentine bodies twisted together like snakes, schools of thrashing sharks, stinging jellyfish, enormous octopi, and two-headed eels with glistening fangs.

All interesting, but not what he was looking for. He could sense Porter's frustration as well. He turned his attention to the map's geologic features. Bloody Blister Bay, Relic Run, Tsunami Shores, Hurricane Hell, Skeleton Harbor, Poison Gull Beach.

Not exactly exciting places to vacation. Nor was there anything there that might show them the way to Arx. Blocked again. His father's maps had been so easy to read. But this one, this was like prying open something that had been sealed shut for centuries. His right wrist—the one that had been grabbed by the scavenger's claw—began to burn and sting.

Refusing to give up, Tom closed his eyes and focused his thoughts on the book. After a moment he felt odd. A current swept through him and the southwestern corner of the map began to glow. Subtle at first, it grew stronger and stronger, turning that portion of the map from a murky blue to a bright pinkish-orange, a color remarkably similar to the folly's rattle in his pocket.

The sea parted slightly, giving them a glimpse of jagged canyon walls just beneath the surface. As he watched, two spiked peaks rose up out of the sea like glistening coral pillars. Fierce, whistling wind whipped between them. The narrow passage shimmered and shook, clearly indicating their way forward.

Victory surged through Tom. He withdrew his fingers from the map at the same instant Porter did.

"There," Porter said, not bothering to mask his triumph. "We'll enter the Cursed Souls Sea there, through that passage."

Willa leapt from her chair and traced a path on a nautical map mounted to the wall. "We're almost there," she announced breathlessly. "Look! We're in the southern straits now. If we veer west—"

"Wait just a blasted minute," Umbrey interrupted. "We're not veering anywhere."

"What do you mean?" Willa asked. "You saw the map, it said to go that way."

"I don't care what the map said. I'm captain of this vessel, and I'm saying we can't. Not in this ship. Ask it to show you another way."

"But—"

"Do it."

Tom and Porter exchanged a look, then did as Umbrey instructed. The result was exactly the same. As the rest of the map went still, a pair of glistening coral pillars rose in the southwestern corner of the map.

Umbrey sighed and drew a hand across the thick stubble covering his chin. "I was afraid of that."

"Afraid of what?" Tom asked.

"That channel there. The Coral Canyon. It's a bottleneck."

Willa looked at Umbrey, her brows drawn together in confusion. "A bottleneck? What does that mean?"

"It means this." Umbrey reached for the desk and grabbed a sheet of paper and a quill. He dipped the quill's tip in ink, then slashed out a rough figure resembling an hourglass. "From the outside, the canyon looks broad enough. But here . . ." He pointed to the middle of the hourglass. "That's where it'll get you. The worst of the coral lurks underwater, sharp as a razor's edge, right where the current's the strongest and the wind does nothing but push you forward. It's a trap, pure and simple. It'll chew us up and spit us out."

Tom remembered the way Umbrey's ship had bumped the gates of Divino as it had sailed past. The *Purgatory's* hull was thick and wide. Sturdy. A vessel built to carry cargo over long ocean voyages, not dart through narrow channels. "So there's no way through?"

Umbrey shook his head. "I've heard too many stories of what happened to those who dared try it. There's no way in. Not in this vessel."

"Wait a minute," Mudge interrupted. "Others have tried to find the Book of Pernicus?"

"No, not the book. Salamaine's treasure. The gold he originally set out to find."

"So that wasn't just a rumor devised to rid his kingdom of dark-haired boys? The gold does exist?" Mudge pressed.

"I assume so." Umbrey pursed his lips in thought. "But—"

"But it doesn't matter," Porter broke in. "We're after the book, not gold." He looked at Umbrey. "What about your rowboats? Those would fit through the channel, right?"

"A rowboat?" Umbrey let out a grim bark of laughter. "You wouldn't last ten minutes. The sea's too rough. It'd swallow you whole."

"You're saying there's no way through?" Porter pressed.

"I'm saying, show me another way and I'll get you there. Just not that way."

Heavy silence fell over the room as they stared at the map, as though expecting it to yield an answer to their dilemma.

Tom shifted slightly, and as he did his hand brushed his jeans pocket. The warmth of the folly's rattle heated his fingertips. *Anything*. He could wish for anything . . . but only once. He froze, wracked by indecision. They needed it, but so did he. His stomach churned as he tried to rationalize away all the reasons he should just keep quiet and hang onto the rattle. After all, they'd never know he even had the thing if he didn't tell them.

But he would know.

And if they failed, Keegan would remain on the loose and scavengers would take over the Five Kingdoms. It would haunt him for the rest of his life. He heaved a sigh (goodbye NBA team, lifetime snowboarding passes, and million dollar lotto ticket), and said, "I think I might have a way for us to get through that canyon."

He set the folly's rattle on top of the map.

Willa drew in a sharp breath and staggered backward. Porter jerked back as well, then swung around to glare at Tom. Only Mudge moved toward the folly's rattle. He leaned forward, examining it closely. "Is that real?"

"Yeah. It is."

Tom heard the note of pride in his voice, but figured he could be forgiven a little swagger. After all, he had single-handedly fought the vicious folly to which the rattle once belonged. He *earned* it. He had every right to keep it for himself. Instead, in a gesture of selfless generosity—extreme selfless generosity— he was willing to give up his own dreams and use it to get the *Purgatory* through the Coral Crater.

He fixed a small smile on his face and looked around the room, waiting to receive their effusive showers of admiration and gratitude.

"Are you crazy? What's wrong with you? What are you thinking, hanging on to something like that?" This, from Porter.

"Don't touch it, Mudge!" shouted Willa as she yanked back the boy's hand.

"I thought I told you to get rid of that blasted thing!" roared Umbrey.

Tom blinked. "*Get rid of it?* Are you kidding me?" He stared at them. He gestured to the folly's rattle. "That's it, that's our answer! All I have to do is wish—""NO!" they shouted in unison, lunging toward him as though they were going to slam their hands over his mouth. "Don't say it!"

Tom looked around the room, then narrowed his gaze at

Umbrey. "What is this? You told me I could wish for anything and it would be granted."

"Aye, but at a cost," Umbrey reminded him. "Always at a cost. Wishes are dangerous things. I told you that, too."

"You wish us through that channel," Porter said, "and there's a good chance we'll end up sinking to the bottom of it."

Tom shook his head. "That doesn't make any sense. Either my wish is granted, or it's not."

"It's not that simple," Willa said. Willa studied the rattle with a look of stark revulsion. "You see, follies are tricky creatures. They have an uncanny sense of knowing what their opponent is going to do next. That's why their rattles are so rare."

Tom thought about that. In his brief battle with the creature, the folly had guessed his every move well before he'd made it. Looking back on it, he wondered if the only reason he'd managed to slice off its rattle was because he had thought he was aiming for its throat.

"Go on," he said to Willa.

"The same is true of granting wishes. That folly is still your opponent. Don't fool yourself into believing he's not. He'll know what you're thinking deep inside and find some way to use your wish against you."

Porter crossed his arms over his chest and studied Tom. "If you don't believe us, just look what happened to Midas."

"Midas? You mean, like King Midas? The guy with the Midas touch?"

"Aye, the very one. A brash man," Umbrey said, shaking his head in disgust. "A greedy one, too. Hadn't held the folly's rattle in his hand for more than thirty seconds when he wished that everything he touched would turn to gold. He got his wish. He couldn't eat—his favorite foods turned to chunks of gold. He couldn't sleep—his warm, soft bed turned to a hardened slab of gold. In the end, he died a broken-hearted man when his beloved daughter turned to a golden statue in his embrace."

Tom slowly digested that. "All right," he said. "So this wishing stuff is tricky. Got it. But maybe if I'm very careful—"

"Forget it," Porter interrupted. "Like I told you before, we don't need you to save us. Quit playing hero. You'll only make things worse."

"Are you serious?" Tom's annoyance with his brother took on a deeper, sharper edge. "Look, I don't know what your problem—"

The rest of his words were lost when a thunderous boom rocked the cabin. Chairs toppled over. Lanterns, ink wells, and sheaves of paper slid from the desk and crashed to the floor. Tom grabbed the edge of the table to steady himself. Willa stumbled into Porter, Mudge hit the floor.

Only Umbrey, with his one good leg, managed to remain fully upright. Cursing soundly, he roared out of the cabin and shot up the ladder to the main deck. Tom stuffed the folly's rattle back in his pocket. Porter grabbed the map of the Cursed Souls Sea, rolled it up, and tucked it inside his shirt. Together they raced after Umbrey, with Willa and Mudge sprinting right behind them.

The shrill clatter of bells greeted them on deck. Crewmen dashed back and forth through a thick haze of acrid smoke. The ear-splitting boom of cannon fire rang out all around them. Until that moment, Tom had no idea how deafening the roar of cannons could be. How the bitter clouds of gunpowder could sting his eyes and clog his throat, totally disorienting him.

In the middle of the chaos, Tom heard a high-pitched whistle bearing straight toward him. He hit the deck, knocking Willa and Mudge down with him. Porter dropped to his belly a second later. A cannonball tore through the heavy canvas sail directly over their heads. It landed in the water on the opposite side of the hull, sending a heavy spray of saltwater pouring down on them.

Then, without warning, a cease-fire. Whoever had been firing on them abruptly stopped.

"Stand down!" Umbrey roared to his crew. "Hold your fire!" He stormed across the deck and snatched a spyglass from a crewman's hand. "Give me that. Let's see what we're up against."

The smoke and haze slowly cleared. The *Purgatory* pitched and rolled as the helmsman tried to maneuver the bulky vessel into a battle-ready position.

Tom rose to his feet and gazed out across the starboard side. As he watched, a three-masted ship drifted out from behind a floating mass of trees. The vessel was entirely red. Billowing red sails, sleek red hull, and polished red decks.

The ship didn't move like Umbrey's vessel, or like any other ship Tom had ever seen. It was smaller, quicker, almost cat-like in its maneuverability. It strutted across the water, taunting the *Purgatory* with its lithe grace. Then it swung around, its cannon bearing directly down on Umbrey and his crew, taking up a position of unmistakable hostility.

Tom braced himself for the impact of artillery. But the ship held its fire. Instead of shooting at them, it hoisted a large black flag with a single red palm print in the center of the cloth off the stern.

Although he had no idea what the flag signaled, Umbrey's men obviously did. The presence of the flag drew a harsh and immediate response. All around him, the crew erupted, swearing and shouting, and violently shaking their fists at the other vessel.

"No sacrifice!"

"We'll take 'em down with us!"

"Rather dead than bled!"

Rather dead than bled? Tom shot a glance at Willa and Mudge, who gripped the ship's rail so tightly their knuckles went white. Beside them, Porter surveyed the flag with a look of dread.

"What is it?" Tom asked

"They've raised a flag of sacrifice. Penalty for trespassing on these waters." Porter swallowed hard, then gestured to the other ship. "They'll allow us to pass, but only for a fee."

"What sort of fee?"

Porter gestured to the red palm print. "The four fingers on that flag means he's asking for four sacrifices. It's called bleeding the crew. He wants Umbrey to give up four crewmen as fee for our passage through these waters."

Tom looked at the sleek red vessel. He definitely didn't want to ask the next question, but he did anyway. "What happens to the four crewmen who are sent over?"

Willa turned toward Tom. Normally, in the bright light of day, her hazel eyes danced with shades of gold and green. Now that light was extinguished.

"That's a slaver," she said, nodding toward the red ship. "Any crewmen Umbrey sacrifices will be sold at the next port and spend the rest of their lives as slaves."

"*What?*" Tom tried to digest the horror of Willa's words, but before he could fully come to terms with them, a single blast rang out. A cannonball landed in the water just a few yards shy of the hull. "What was that?" he said.

"They're marking time," Porter answered. "A minute has passed since the slaver raised his flag. Umbrey has four more minutes to decide who he'll sacrifice."

"And if he refuses?"

"Then they'll start firing for real," Porter replied. "They won't stop until they've blown us out of the water. Most everyone will be killed. Any who survive will be taken prisoner and sold as slaves. If Umbrey can't make a choice, the choice will be made for him."

Mudge lifted the Sword of Five Kingdoms and rested it lightly against the rail. His expression troubled, he traced his finger lightly over the blade and murmured softly, "The sacrifice of a few innocents, for the lives of many."

Tom froze. He looked at Mudge, at the sword, at the red ship. . . . The glimmer of an idea shot through his mind, but he wasn't fast enough to grasp it. There was a solution there, right there, if he could just *think*.

The sacrifice of a few innocents, for the lives of many.

Wasn't that the lesson in the tale of Salamaine's curse? The sacrifice of innocents hadn't worked for Salamaine, so it wouldn't work for them.

A second cannonball exploded through the air.

Three more minutes.

"They're waiting for an answer," said the crewman to Umbrey's right. "Should I give the word to open fire, cap'n?"

Umbrey lowered his spyglass. He gave a small shake of his head. "He's carrying cargo."

Tom squinted across the water. *Human* cargo. The lower deck was crowded with men, women, and children—some of them so young they had to be held up to see over the edge of the ship's rail.

Umbrey's lips formed a thin, tight line. "I've never fired on a ship carrying women and children, and I'm not about to start now."

"Can we outrun them?" Willa asked.

"A ship like that?" Umbrey said, giving a harsh laugh. "No. That vessel was built for speed—speed and treacherous seas. We don't stand a chance against it."

A third cannonball rocketed through the air.
Two more minutes.

"Fire the engines!" Umbrey roared to his crew. He drew himself up, squared his shoulders, and gave a decisive nod. "Right. So that's it then. No sacrifices. I won't bleed my crew. I won't fire upon a slaver carrying cargo. And we can't outrun them—but we'll try. We may not get far, but at least we'll give them a run for their money."

"Wait!" Tom shouted. "That's it!" He couldn't grasp it before, but suddenly everything was perfectly clear. "We can't run *from* the ship, so we've got to run *toward* it. We'll go! The four of us!"

"*What?*" Porter stared at him in horror. "What are you talking about?"

"*That ship!* Don't you see? It's perfect. That's the ship we need to make it through the Coral Canyon."

Willa's jaw dropped open. She whipped around and looked at the ship, then she looked back at Tom. "You think . . . "

"Absolutely. We go, but not as sacrifices. We get aboard and *take* the ship," Tom said. "That's our only solution."

"*Take* the ship?" Porter gave a hollow laugh. "And how are we supposed to do that?"

"I don't know yet," he admitted. "We'll have to figure it out."

"Right. We'll just *figure out* how to overtake the highly-trained, heavily-armed crew of a slave ship and seize the vessel."

"He didn't say it would be easy," Mudge pointed out.

The forth and final cannonball shot through the air.
Sixty seconds left.

"The Black Book of Pernicus," Tom said. "We can find it. We've got the sword, the map, and that's the ship we need to get through the channel. It's *right there.*" Sensing he was gaining, he pressed, "We can't just sit here and wait to be blown apart. We have to do it. If you have a better idea, tell me now. No, tell me *ten seconds ago*, because that's when I needed to hear it."

Porter ground his teeth, clenching his fists at his side. He let out a deep growl of frustration and glared at Tom. "You realize what will happen if we fail."

"Who said anything about failing?"

"Now there's the spirit!" Umbrey cried. "The game's not over yet!" He turned and roared across the deck, "Kill the engines and ready the dinghy! Four going over!"

They raced across the deck and leapt into a wooden lifeboat hanging off the outer side of the hull. Umbrey watched them settle in. "You know what they say, lads. A bold beginning is half the battle."

"Perfect," Porter bit out. "Another idiotic scheme. We've got no chance."

"No chance?" Umbrey echoed, appalled. "Are you daft, lad? You're still alive! That's a raging success in my book. Better than how things stood thirty seconds ago. By my way of looking at it, your future's already brighter."

Umbrey signaled to his crewman. The man released the ropes which held the dinghy aloft. It plummeted straight down, hitting the water with a splash. The instant the boat settled, Umbrey sent them a thumbs-up and a beaming smile. "Victory, lads! Victory!"

Tom tried to smile back, but couldn't quite manage it. He looked from Porter to Willa to Mudge, all of whom stared back at him with varying expressions of terror, doubt, and (in Porter's case) outright hostility.

There was no turning back now. Tom picked up the oars and began rowing toward the slave ship.

CHAPTER ELEVEN

CRIMSON BELLE

They weren't alone in the water. At first Tom thought the boat had landed in a thick nest of drifting kelp. Then he sensed a subtle vibration within the water, a deliberate thrashing movement that could not be attributed to the current. He stilled his oars and peered over the side.

Swimming and swirling all around them were dozens of long, wiry, amphibian-looking creatures. Their skin was mottled green, as slick and slimy as seaweed, with occasional patches of bumpy warts. Their limbs were bent, their hands and feet webbed, and a scaly crown was affixed to their skulls in place of hair. But the most disturbing thing about them was their nearly human faces. They stared up at Tom with dark bulgy eyes, their broad mouths curved in leering grins.

"What are those things?" he asked, barely managing to repress a shudder.

"Undertoads," replied Mudge.

Willa elaborated, "This isn't their natural territory. Usually they're found near beaches, just beyond the wave break, waiting to catch swimmers who venture too far from shore."

"What do you mean by *catch swimmers?*"

"That's how they feed," she said. "They have suction cups

attached to their hands and feet. Once you're caught, there's no escaping them. Even the most powerful swimmer will be pulled under and drown."

Porter drew up one knee and rested his arm across it. "So if part of your plan was for us to leap overboard and swim to safety if things go badly, forget it. Slave ship captains feed scraps to the undertoads every night to make sure they follow their ships. No better way to keep the slaves, and their crews, on board and following orders. But then you knew that already, didn't you?"

Tom didn't miss the haughty challenge in his brother's voice, but he refused to be baited into an argument. "No, I didn't," he said simply. "And I don't have a plan. Not yet."

Porter cut a glance at the red sailing vessel that loomed ominously closer with each stroke of the oars. "Well, this might be a good time to think of one."

"All right." Tom let the oars fall in his lap, allowing the current to direct their boat. "First thing we need to do is figure out what we're up against. How many crew members do you think there are? What kind of weapons they have? I figure there'll be too many of them for us to handle, so we'll need help."

"The slaves," Willa said, nodding thoughtfully.

"Exactly," Tom said. "Once the crew is taken out, the slaves can man the vessel. At least a few of them should have sailing experience, right?"

"Wrong," Porter returned flatly. "The slaves come from Divino. Flatlanders. You'll find no sailors among them. They're criminals mostly."

Tom frowned.

"What sort of criminals?" he asked.

"Men convicted of petty theft, smuggling, or forgery.

Farmers too poor to pay their debts. Drunks who fall asleep on public benches. Women caught stealing food from their neighbors' gardens." Porter shrugged. "Almost anything."

"But there were children there," Tom countered. "*Young* children. What sort of crime could they have committed?"

Porter looked at him as though he were painfully slow. "You saw the courthouse where Keegan was held. Beneath it was a single room for holding prisoners during trial. That's all. No prisons, no jails. Once convicted, prisoners are shipped out, handed over to slavers from Aquat. Their families are sent with them. That's how it works."

"So you're telling me if a man is caught stealing a loaf of bread," Tom said, "his entire family risks being shipped off into slavery?"

"It's meant to keep others from commiting crimes," Willa said softly.

"Keegan's system," Mudge said. His gaze turned toward the red vessel. "But it will end. I will see to it once we return to Divino."

"*If* we make it back," Porter countered grimly. "No one who's ever shipped out on a slaver has ever been seen or heard from again."

Tom swallowed hard. The magnitude of what they'd undertaken —no, what he'd *encouraged* them to undertake—pressed upon him like a great, invisible weight. Maybe Porter was right. Maybe his plan had been a little brash. Supposing for a minute they could overpower the crew (a feat that was looking less likely with every passing second), how exactly were they supposed to navigate their way through the Coral Canyon, then sail across the Cursed Souls Sea?

Tom considered the depth of his own sailing experience. Not exactly promising. The rowboat he'd taken into the Forbidden

Lake had sunk. This morning aboard the *Purgatory* he'd barely been able to figure out how the bathroom worked. The dinghy in which they currently sat was still afloat, but that didn't mean much. The sea was so thick with undertoads, he wouldn't be surprised if their suction cup fingers were accidentally plugging up any holes he might have knocked in the bottom.

Obviously they would need a plan.

"Obviously we'll need a plan," Porter said.

Startled, Tom looked at Porter. He'd heard twins could do that—read each other's thoughts without communicating—but he wasn't sure he liked it. Frankly, he wasn't sure he even liked Porter. The only time he felt at all connected to his brother was when they brought maps to life.

"*My* plan," Porter said, leveling his pale gaze directly at Tom. "Not some idiotic, shoot-off-my-mouth-so-I-can-look-like-a-hero plan that only puts us in more danger than we were in five minutes ago. Let's try something intelligent for a change, shall we?"

Actually, Tom was pretty convinced he didn't like Porter at all.

"Fine," he shot back, meeting his brother's frigid glare. "You want to be in charge, you figure it all out. You let me know when you do."

"Right. How very predictable. You get us into this mess, then leave it to me to figure out how to get us out."

"What are you talking about? If I hadn't—"

"Stop it, both of you!" Willa cut in. "We don't have time for this!"

Their lifeboat bumped up against the slave ship's hull. A rope ladder sailed over the rail and splashed into the water beside them, a silent invitation to climb aboard.

For a moment, no one spoke. No one moved. Then Porter let out a deep breath. "I guess it's a little too late to turn back now, isn't it?"

One of Professor Lost's lectures echoed back to Tom. Courage did not mean being unafraid. Courage meant being terrified, but going forward anyway.

Moving carefully so he wouldn't tip their boat, he eased himself into a standing position and grabbed the rope ladder. He swung his legs onto the bottom rung.

"Wait," Porter said.

Tom turned. "What?"

Porter hesitated for a moment, a muscle working in his cheek. Finally he gave a curt nod and said, "Good luck."

Tom nodded back. He looked at Porter, then at Willa and Mudge. "We'll be fine. All of us. We've been in worse spots before."

As he climbed up the rope ladder he wondered if that was true. There was no time to mull it over. The moment he reached the ship's rail two burly crewmen grabbed his upper arms and dragged him off the ladder. They tossed him on the deck as though he weighed little more than a sack of potatoes. He stumbled backward but caught himself before he fell. Willa came next, then Mudge and Porter, who were all pitched aboard in the same rough way Tom had been.

Tom had thought Umbrey's crew was a rough-looking bunch. He revised that impression. They were as threatening as Santa's elves compared to the men who surrounded him now.

These were enormous, barrel-chested men, a good head-and-a-half taller than he was, with thighs as solid as the ship's mast and bulging biceps that glistened with sweat. He immediately discarded any idiotic fantasy that he might be able to physically overpower the crew. Porter hesitated for a moment, chewing the inside of his jaw.

He studied their faces as they patted him down—searching for weapons, he assumed—but saw nothing in their glacial stares that might suggest pity for his plight. In fact, just the opposite was true. They were entirely indifferent. The moment he stepped aboard he became cargo. Nothing more, nothing less.

"Hey! That's mine!"

Tom's gaze shot to Porter. His brother lunged for the rolled parchment that had been found within his coat. As one crewman opened the map of the Cursed Souls Sea and studied it curiously, another shoved Porter back, the crewman's broad hand splayed open against Porter's chest.

"Give it here," said a deep voice from behind them.

A man strode into the fray. For a long moment, Tom could do nothing but look at him, so striking was his appearance. Physically, he was as enormous as the rest of the crewmen, but that was where his resemblance to anyone else on board stopped.

The man reminded Tom of an Arabian sultan. Rather than outfitting himself in working attire, he wore a pair of bright purple, pantaloon-style silk pants and pointy red slippers, with a tiny bell affixed to the toe of each slipper. An emerald green, fringed belt wrapped around his waist, into which he'd tucked an enormous curved blade. His chest was bare, showing a broad expanse of mahogany skin and bulging muscles. A thick gold chain draped around his neck, from which was suspended an ornate golden orb roughly half the size of Tom's fist. On his shoulder rode a large, deep crimson bird. When it ruffled its feathers, it shimmered like a living flame.

The man positioned himself in front of them with the map of the Cursed Souls Sea curled in his fist. He studied them with dark, cold eyes.

"Listen well, for I will only say this once. You are now aboard the *Crimson Belle*. I am Salvador Zaputo, captain of this ship and ruler of Aquat. Disobey my orders, and you will die. Strike one of my crewmen, and you will die. Try to escape, and you will die. Is this clear?"

Not a lot of room for interpretation there.

Tom swallowed hard and nodded, as did Porter, Willa, and Mudge.

Satisfied, Zaputo transferred his attention to the rolled

parchment. "The Cursed Souls Sea," he said, his dark gaze moving across the map. He scowled at Porter. "Why do you have this?"

Porter froze. Tom could see his brother thinking, assessing their situation. Apparently determining to stick as close to the truth as possible, he said, "We need to travel there. There's something we must find and return to Divino."

The man's gaze narrowed. "Something? What do you search for?"

Again, Porter hesitated. Again, he determined to stick to the truth. "A book."

For a long moment, Zaputo just stared at him. Then his lips split into a broad grin. He let out a shout of laughter, but his eyes were serious. "I hope it was a good book, for you and your friends have just traded your lives for it."

Turning away from Porter, he nodded to his men. "What about the others?"

Tom had already been searched. The crewmen now turned to Willa and Mudge. One crewman jerked the cloth satchel from Willa's shoulder and tossed it to his leader. Another gave Mudge a cursory patting down.

Tom stiffened, horrified the man might discover the Sword of Five Kingdoms. Mudge caught Tom's eye and gave a slight shake of his head, then flicked his forefinger toward his boot, indicating without words where he'd hidden it.

"What is this?" Zaputo boomed as he pawed through Willa's satchel.

"Herbs," she said. "Medicines, balms, and the like."

Zaputo carelessly pitched it back to her. "Worthless." Then his eyes narrowed as he surveyed them suspiciously. "You came from the *Purgatory*. Umbrey's ship. He is rumored to be a man of honor. A lie. He gave up his crew without a fight."

"We're not crew," Willa said. "We . . . stowed away."

Zaputo considered that for a moment, then seemed to accept it. "You picked the wrong ship to hide in," he sneered. "Just as I thought. The people of Divino have no honor. They will give away their own children if it saves their skins."

Mudge, who had remained silent until that moment, stepped forward. "Salvador Zaputo," he said. "I've heard of you."

Surprise flashed across Zaputo's face. He looked Mudge up and down. His lips curved in a smile of cruel condescension. "Oh? Is my reputation so fierce? Do I strike fear in the hearts of little children? Does my very name give you nightmares?"

Refusing to be baited by his words, Mudge said calmly, "You have children of your own."

Zaputo puffed out his chest. "Five," he said. "Three sons and two daughters."

"You say the people of Divino won't fight," Mudge continued. "Tell me about the people of Aquat. What would you do if your children were threatened?"

Rage darkened Zaputo's eyes. He leaned down, bringing his face inches away from Mudge's. He hung there for a long, tense moment, then he roared out, *"I would fight for them!"*

Mudge seemed to consider that. His young face glowed with satisfaction as he gave a solemn nod. "Good."

Zaputo frowned, apparently disconcerted by his inability to intimidate Mudge the way he'd meant to. His gaze locked on Mudge for another beat, as though trying to figure him out, then he straightened to his full height and gave an impatient shake of his head. "Ridiculous. I've wasted enough time talking with children." He nodded to one of his crewmen, saying as he turned to leave, "Get rid of them when we dock at Vespa tomorrow night."

"Wait!" Porter called out, stepping after him. "My map."

He'd barely gotten the words out when Zaputo spun around. Using just one hand, he caught Porter by the front of his shirt and lifted him off his feet. With his other hand, he raised the rolled parchment. "*My* map," he said. "*My* ship. *My* cargo. You and your friends belong to me now. Don't forget it again." He released Porter abruptly, shoving him back into the bulwark.

Before Tom could think of what to do, or react in any way, Zaputo's crewmen herded them toward the ship's stern, back to the crowded deck where the rest of the captives waited.

Icy panic shot through Tom's veins. They'd made it aboard the *Crimson Belle*. But unless he could think of something fast—*really* fast, considering Vespa was apparently less than twenty-four hours away—they'd be sold as slaves the moment the ship docked.

CHAPTER TWELVE

POOR PLANNING

"The folly's rattle," Tom whispered to Porter. "It's our only way out."

Through carelessness on the part of Zaputo's crew when they frisked him—or perhaps because the four of them hadn't looked threatening enough to warrant a thorough search—Tom still had the rattle in his pocket.

Porter shook his head. "Too risky," he whispered back. "We'll save it as a last resort, and only if we get the wording exactly right."

Tom ground his teeth in frustration at Porter's stubborn refusal to use the wish. Did it really matter if he got the wording exactly right? Wasn't avoiding spending the rest of their lives as slaves a little bit more important?

It was late. Past midnight, Tom guessed, though there was no way for him to really know. He glanced overhead. The stars had shifted, but that meant little to him. He wasn't good enough at reading the movement of constellations to understand how they marked time. As he'd seen aboard the *Purgatory*, Zaputo's crew changed shifts at the ringing of the bells. But again, Tom wasn't sure how that corresponded to actual time. He only knew the constant clamor, combined with driving panic over their situation, kept him awake.

That wasn't true for everyone else aboard. Their snores and grunts filled the air. He glanced across the deck. He estimated there were at least one hundred captives aboard, all crowded together on the aft deck. Mostly men, though there were a good number of women and children among them as well. Perhaps one or two of the captives had the menacing air of hardened criminals. The majority were average citizens of Divino who'd been down on their luck, caught in the wrong place at the wrong time.

Their sentences varied. Some were to spend the rest of their lives slaving in the ice mines of Ventus, others would work the fiery forges of Incendia, and still others would labor in the deadly jungles of Terrum. What troubled Tom most was how they accepted their fate. They had abandoned all hope of changing their futures.

His gaze turned to Willa and Mudge. They were sitting up, just as he and Porter were, with their backs resting against the rail. Somehow, despite their uncomfortable position, they'd both managed to fall asleep.

Tom's stomach clenched as he studied them. If he failed and couldn't find a way to take control of the ship, or at the very least find a way off it, whatever happened next would be his fault. He pushed the morbid thought away, refusing to give up. As Umbrey had said, the game wasn't over yet.

He glanced upward. The red sails of the *Crimson Belle* worked to render her nearly invisible at night—he could barely make them out billowing directly over his head. The same wouldn't be true of the *Purgatory*, however.

For perhaps the hundredth time since boarding the slaver, he scanned the horizon, searching for a glimmer of white sails reflected in the moonlit sea. Nothing. No indication that the *Purgatory* was still in the vicinity. For all Tom knew, Umbrey could have cast them off in the dinghy and just sailed away to safety.

He leaned in closer to Porter. "You think Umbrey is still out there?"

"I've been looking. I haven't seen him," Porter said.

"But he wouldn't have just left us."

"Forget that. Listen. I have a plan."

Porter's gaze shot around the deck. The crewmen Zaputo had posted as guards stood at a distance of several feet, but at the moment they faced away from them. In the hours Tom had been aboard the *Crimson Belle*, he'd witnessed no overt cruelty on the part of Zaputo and his men. But neither had they shown any sympathy. They provided food, water, and nothing else, moving about the ship with expressions of stoic indifference, as though the transport of human beings to forced labor camps was an unpleasant but necessary chore.

"I've worked everything out. We storm the helm at daybreak when they bring our morning meal," Porter said. "I've been watching. Most of the crew goes below deck to eat at the same time they bring our food. Things are most unsettled then. If we all rush out together and charge them—"

"Wait a minute. All? Who's all?"

"Every man here." Porter said. "We may not have weapons, but we outnumber them by four-to-one. If we charge them together we have a chance."

"A chance? A chance to do what?"

"Take over the *Crimson Belle*," Porter snapped. "What else? That's the whole point. That's why we're here. We storm the crew, lock Zaputo and his men in the cargo hold, and take over the ship. We'll sail it through the Cursed Souls Sea ourselves."

Tom stared at Porter, not sure where to begin. In the first place, even supposing that by some miracle they were able to overtake Zaputo's men—and now that he'd seen them up close, he put those odds at slim to none—how were they supposed to navigate their way through one of the most treacherous passes in the Cursed Souls Sea? It didn't make sense.

Tom took a shaky breath, searching for the right words. Granted, he had a brash style of his own (acting first, thinking later) but he didn't see Porter's way of doing things (hitting as hard as he could at anything that got in his way, Tom included), was necessarily better. His plan had failure written all over it. At the same time, they had to do *something*.

His gaze traveled once again to Willa and Mudge. They might have thought of something he and Porter hadn't. He didn't want to draw too much attention to himself now, but he could talk to Willa in the morning. If she'd come up with a smarter approach, it was worth waiting to hear about. She still had her bag of herbs. What if she had a sleeping powder they could give to the crew to knock them out—wouldn't that be a whole lot smarter than trying to overpower them?

"Maybe if we wait and talk to Willa . . . " he ventured cautiously.

Porter's face tightened. "No. There's no time to wait. For once, we do this *my* way, not yours. I've already spread the word. These men and I will storm the crew tomorrow morning at dawn. If you don't want to help us, you can stay here and wait with the women and children."

"You there!" bellowed one of the crewmen, glaring at Porter. "Quiet!"

Porter abruptly turned away, presenting his back to Tom.

Tom clenched his fists and stared at him for a long moment, then he tipped his head back and looked to the starry sky. He studied the heavens without seeing them, his focus too absorbed by the dark emotions brewing within him. He silently swore at his brother, calling him every vile name he could think of. Then a different kind of emotion settled over him.

Despair.

At daybreak, Porter was going to get himself killed. The

men who followed him would likely be killed as well. Porter's plan wouldn't work. Tom *knew* it wouldn't work. But he could think of nothing he could do to stop it.

The night dragged slowly past. Tom rested, but couldn't sleep. Instead he drifted in and out through a cloudy haze of exhaustion, worry, and uncertainty.

Finally the stars dimmed, their brilliant pinpricks of light becoming paler and paler until they were completely extinguished. A soft lavender glow lit the edges of the horizon. The sun, like a fiery ball tossed up from the depths of the sea, slowly rose.

Dawn had arrived.

In the distance, Tom heard the shuffle of Zaputo's crew, followed by the clatter of tin pots being scraped empty. Breakfast. A line of crewmen approached, bearing enormous trays laden with plates of food.

Beside him, Porter shifted slightly, drawing one knee up in a position that would allow him to spring to his feet. He dragged in a deep breath and let it out slowly, as though bracing himself.

Tom tensed. Dread, as thick and heavy as soured milk, filled his mouth. His stomach churned. His heart beat at triple its normal rate.

"Wait," he whispered.

Porter shook him off.

The first of Zaputo's crewman waded into their midst.

Porter shot to his feet. Letting out a defiant roar, he lowered his head and charged like a bull, driving his shoulder into the man's gut. The breakfast tray, along with all the plates atop it, crashed to the ground. The man staggered backward. He fell over, bringing Porter down with him.

All around Tom, captives leapt to their feet, their voices

raised in fury as they rushed the crew.

The fight for the *Crimson Belle* had begun.

Tom dove into the fray. It didn't occur to him to do anything else. Not when the fight was erupting on all sides of him with fists flying, bodies tumbling, and skulls cracking. Tom wasn't sure he could even call it a fight. It was more like a prison riot.

Zaputo's men were enormous, their bodies solid walls of muscle. But they were outnumbered by four-to-one. And while the captives had no weapons, they brought something even more important to the battle: the savage desperation of men who had nothing to lose. In the end, it was a simple matter of fight or die.

The brawl spilled out of the aft deck where the captives were held. A few combatants tumbled and rolled across the deck, their fingers clenched around each other's throats. Others swung at the crewmen with trays, bowls, ropes—anything they could get their hands on.

One of Zaputo's men lashed his sword at Tom. Tom twisted past him, but barely. The man's blade caught his coarse linen overshirt, the one he'd borrowed from Umbrey's crew, and ripped it open from hem to throat. Tom spun away, sending the man stumbling with a vicious kick to his knee. He weaved through the sprawling chaos, pitching himself into the fight.

Through the blur of battle, Tom saw Porter slammed to the ground. The crewman Porter had initially knocked down was now positioned above him with his fist raised, ready to deliver a teeth-shattering blow. Tom leapt toward him in a flying tackle. He caught the man in the shoulder, shoving him hard into the wooden deck. The diversionary tactic worked, but not for long.

The man was up in an instant, this time swinging at Tom. Tom ducked, but he wasn't fast enough. The man's fist connected with his ear. Tom's vision went black and the world spun, the ground shooting out from beneath him. He hit the deck face-first. The taste of blood filled his mouth.

He shook his head to clear it. From the corner of his eye, he caught a glimpse of a golden braid shoot past him, followed by a dark-haired boy. Willa and Mudge. Tom bit back a groan. He'd assumed Willa had fled the battle and taken Mudge away with the other captive children to hide somewhere safe. An idiotic assumption. He'd never seen either of them run from trouble.

Sure enough, Willa charged headlong into the fight, furiously swinging her bag of herbs over her head. She let the bag fly, aiming for the crewman who'd punched Tom. It hit him squarely in the throat, sending an explosion of powders and herbs up into his face. The man coughed and wheezed, temporarily blinded. He staggered backward.

A rope dangled from the main mast. Porter grabbed it with both hands and swung around hard, raising his feet to kick the man squarely in the chest. Mudge ducked down behind the crewman as Porter's boots struck. The man went flying backward, toppling between decks and tumbling down a hatch leading to a lower level.

For one brief, incredible moment, Tom sensed the momentum shift in their favor. He dragged himself up on all fours and looked around. A smile of pure, astonished joy curved his lips. A painful smile, for he felt his swollen lower lip crack and bleed at that slight motion. It didn't matter. They were winning. Now all they had to do—

An explosion rocked the air around them. A cannonball tore through their midst, sailing across the deck just inches above Tom's head. He instinctively went flat, as did every other man, woman, and child caught up in the fray.

"Enough!" roared Salvador Zaputo.

Zaputo stood with his scimitar sword raised at his side. His fiery bird rested on his shoulder, its flame-colored feathers shimmering in the early morning sun. Flanking Zaputo on both sides were the remainder of his crew, at least two dozen strong, all armed with swords.

Five cannons had been rolled into position between Zaputo and his men. One, presumably the one that had just been fired, belched out smoke. The remaining four were primed and loaded, their fuses ready to be lit. Those were aimed directly at the captives.

Tom froze, as did everyone around him.

"I see you've chosen this morning to die," Zaputo said, shattering the tense silence that had fallen over the ship. "Very well. I shall grant your wish." His dark eyes scanned the crowded deck. "Bring me the four who came aboard yesterday. We will begin with them."

CHAPTER THIRTEEN

MANA SEED

Before Tom could move, or even *think* about moving, two of Zaputo's crewmen grabbed his upper arms and jerked him to his feet and dragged him forward. Porter, Willa, and Mudge each received the same ruthless handling. The crewmen shoved them against the rough wood of a bulwark, pinning their backs against it and holding them there.

"You were warned," Zaputo said. "We had peace until you came aboard. You attacked my crew. The punishment is death."

Four crewman stepped forward, their swords raised. Shock and disbelief tore through Tom. It couldn't end. Not like this. He heard Willa's gasp of distress, Porter's dark oath, Mudge's cry of, "Wait! Listen!"

But there was no waiting, no listening.

"It was all my idea!" Tom burst out. "I started the fight! Not them!"

Zaputo looked at Tom. "You?"

"Yes! Me! They were against the idea. They told me it was foolish and they were right."

"No!" Porter shouted, but he was too late. Now that Tom had Zaputo's attention, he wasn't going to stop.

"Don't kill them," Tom said. "It was all my idea."

Zaputo studied him for a moment, then nodded. "So be it."

Tom struggled to break free, but his movements only caused Zaputo's men to tighten their grip on his upper arms. As though witnessing events unfold from very far away, he watched as a crewman brought his blade to rest just above his heart. The razor-sharp tip of the sword pierced the thin cotton of his tee shirt.

He closed his eyes, bracing himself for the searing thrust of the blade.

"You are not the man you claim to be," Mudge burst out. "The ruler of Aquat is said to be a man of honor. You're nothing but a murderer!"

Tom's eyes flew open. He stared at Mudge in horror as Zaputo's face darkened with fury.

Zaputo stopped. Turned. Looked at Mudge. "What did you say?"

"He didn't mean it!" Porter shouted. "He's confused! He doesn't know—"

"Silence!" roared Zaputo. He laid his fingertips on the blade and lowered it, turning the sword away from Tom's chest. Then he stepped toward Mudge. Softly he growled, "I would like to hear this child speak. This child who would dare to insult me in front of my crew."

Porter shot Mudge a look of warning. A look which Mudge ignored.

"You fill your ship with human cargo. You earn your money selling the men, women, and children of Divino. Have you no pity?"

"Pity for the people of Divino?" Zaputo scoffed. The fiery bird riding on his shoulder let out a sharp *caw!* as though joining Zaputo in mocking Mudge's words. Zaputo slowly shook his head. "Let me show you how the people of Divino treat their brothers in Aquat."

He lifted the thick gold chain he wore around his neck and reached for the ornate golden orb which dangled from the end. His fingers found a tiny, sensitive trigger. Like an over-sized locket, the orb sprang open to reveal a hollow interior. Nestled inside was a small, shriveled object that resembled a walnut shell. Zaputo removed it and held it between his thumb and forefinger.

"A mana seed," Willa breathed, unable to keep the awe from her voice.

"It *was* a mana seed," Zaputo corrected. "But no longer." He rapped it against the ship's rail, producing the sharp, dry echo of hardened stone. "For centuries, my people were fed with the rich fruit of the mana tree. Our land was prosperous, lush, and beautiful. But one day the seed began to shrivel and die. There was no more fruit. No more food. My people starved. We turned to Divino for help, but they did nothing. *Nothing.* They would have let us starve to death."

"But you didn't starve to death," Porter interjected. "Divino must have helped you in some way."

"Help?" Zaputo's eyes went black. "Your ruler, Keegan, gave me a choice. Use my fleet of ships to ferry his slaves, in return for barely enough food to keep my people from certain starvation, or watch them die. That was how Keegan helped me—by giving me a choice. Do his evil deeds or let my people die. I chose for the people of Aquat to live."

Zaputo took a step back. He planted his legs wide and folded his arms across his broad chest, assuming a stance of contemptuous command. "You ask for pity? There is none. The people of Divino mean nothing to me." He raised the mana seed and held it aloft. "As this seed hardened, so did the hearts of the people of Aquat."

For a long moment there seemed to be nothing to say. Then Mudge spoke.

"You're wrong. Keegan does not use you. You allow yourself

to be used. You are the captive here—Keegan's captive. Today is the day to break free. To choose not to do Keegan's bidding."

Astonishment swept across the harsh lines of Zaputo's face. He gave a low rumble of laughter and glanced over his shoulder at his men. "Bold words for a small child. He chirps like a little bird, filling the air with his noise."

His crewmen joined in the ridicule of Mudge. But as the laughter subsided, Tom noted that something about Zaputo had changed.

A moment ago he'd been ready to order his men to kill them all. Now a glimmer of interest showed in his dark eyes. He studied Mudge with an intensity that went beyond mere cutthroat desire to see him punished for the failed mutiny. A distant spark of recognition lurked in his gaze—a recognition of truth that somehow seemed to play in Mudge's favor.

As though sensing his advantage, Mudge pushed on. "Keegan's days of power are over. The tides have changed. There is a new ruler in Divino."

Zaputo shrugged. "This news has already reached us. It means nothing. The next ruler of Divino will be as evil as Keegan. That will never change."

"You're wrong. The new ruler of Divino will help your people."

The statement was so at odds with the reality of their situation—vastly outnumbered and utterly defenseless—it was hard for Tom not to gawk at Mudge in disbelief.

Zaputo opened his mouth as though he was going to make another biting comment, but his words died in his throat as Mudge reached into his boot and withdrew the Sword of Five Kingdoms, its five black stones glistening in the morning sunlight.

"I tell you this as new ruler of Divino."

Zaputo drew in a sharp breath. His men tensed, reaching for their weapons, but Zaputo stayed them off with a wave of his hand. He stepped forward, intently examining the blade. He glared at Mudge. "The Sword of Five Kingdoms," he said. "What trickery is this?"

"No trickery," Mudge replied. "Proof that I tell you the truth about Keegan. He has been defeated."

Zaputo's brows narrowed. His voice rose. "And now you think you will use that sword to defeat me?"

"No," Mudge answered. "No more battles. No more slave trade. Our people were once united. Our nations prospered. It can be so again, but only if we work together. We can help the people of Aquat. We will find another way to feed your people. Together we will rebuild your proud nation."

Zaputo scratched his chin and regarded Mudge as though he were looking at an utterly confounding creature, a dog that could talk or a sheep that quacked. "Empty promises," he muttered.

"Real promises," Mudge countered. "But first we must rid both our lands of the scavengers. If they've reached Divino, they must be in Aquat as well."

Although Zaputo didn't reply, the dark looks exchanged by his crew, coupled with their uncomfortable shuffling, was answer enough.

"We can destroy them all," Porter cut in. "The Black Book of Pernicus will tell us how. The map we brought aboard, the map of the Cursed Souls Sea, leads us directly to it."

Zaputo's lips curved upward in a cold smile. "The Black Book cannot be found. It has been missing for thousands of years."

"We can find it," Mudge said. "Just as we found this sword. The map you took from us leads to the book. But we'll need your help to reach it."

Willa stepped forward. "You swore yesterday you would fight for your children," she reminded Zaputo. "Now is the time to do so."

Zaputo glared at Willa. Then he turned his dark stare on Tom, Porter, and Mudge.

Tom moved to stand beside Willa. "Everything you've heard is true—"

"Enough!" Zaputo bellowed. "I have heard enough! Now I will think on it."

Tom went still, his pulse hammering in his ears as he waited for Zaputo to decide what to do.

Seconds stretched into what seemed like hours. Tom's senses intensified as the moment seemed to freeze in time. He was aware of the sharp morning breeze snapping the ruby sails overhead, the scent of gunpowder lingering in the air, the anxious shuffle of the captives as they awaited their own fates.

Finally, Zaputo nodded to his crew. "Bring me that map."

Tom's relief was so great his knees nearly buckled. He glanced at his friends, watching as the color rushed back into Willa's ashen face and Porter dragged in a deep, shuddering breath. Mudge was the only one not obviously overcome with relief. Instead, he studied Zaputo with an expression that looked remarkably like approval.

"They will show you where the book can be found," Mudge said, nodding to Tom and Porter.

Two of Zaputo's men dragged a table into place, as another retrieved the map and spread it open.

Tom positioned himself at the western edge of the map, while Porter took the eastern edge. Their gazes locked and they exchanged a nod. Wordlessly they brought their fingertips down to rest on the parchment. The map came to life, drawing gasps from Zaputo and his crew, as well as from the captives who watched from a few yards away.

Tom ignored them all, keeping his focus locked on the map.

While the Cursed Souls Sea remained as violent as ever, and the Coral Canyon showed itself to be the only entrance into that agitated body of water, other things had changed. As they drew closer to the book, the map was somehow adjusting itself to reflect their journey.

The island city of Arx came into view in greater detail. To Tom, it looked as though he was viewing the crumbling remains of a great Roman metropolis, a city which must once have been a thriving center of trade. Within the ruins he recognized an open air amphitheater, a market square, courthouses, and other public buildings. The structures had been built of glistening terracotta stone, giving the whole scene a sparkling, fairytale-like glow.

His gaze moved to the tall, lighthouse-style fortress which jutted up on the northern end of the island. It was there that the Black Book of Pernicus was held. The enormous guards armed with scimitar swords he and Porter had seen earlier—men Tom now recognized as Zaputo's crew—no longer blocked the entrance. But that new advantage was cancelled by something far more difficult to overcome.

The island itself was composed of nearly solid vertical rock walls. There was only one spot on the entire island where a ship could reasonably gain access, a rocky beach a few hundred feet wide. A rocky beach where hordes of moaning, angry, hungry scavengers staggered.

From a distance, it might look like a fairytale kingdom, but it had been completely overrun by the undead. If they wanted to get ashore, they would have to fight their way across hundreds of bloodthirsty scavengers.

Tom and Porter lifted their fingers from the map and stared at each other in dismay.

Impossible.

CHAPTER FOURTEEN

A DANGEROUS BIRD

Tom shook his head, pushing away the exhaustion and defeat that threatened to overwhelm him. It couldn't be impossible. They'd gotten this far, there had to be a way forward. There had to be.

He just didn't know what it was.

He looked up to find Zaputo and his crew watching them intently, their gazes shifting from Tom and Porter to the map resting between them.

"The Hero Twins," Zaputo said, as though slowly connecting the pieces.

Tom didn't much like that description. Probably the last word in the world he'd use to describe himself would be *hero*. Right after that, in a list of words least likely to apply to him, would be the term *cool-headed*. Based on Porter's sour expression, his brother didn't much like the title, either.

"I've heard of you," Zaputo continued gruffly. "The prophecies say you'll bring light back to the Five Kingdoms. Banish the darkness that has plagued us for centuries" and exactly why Tom resisted the title of hero.

The expectations ran just a tad too high for his taste. *Banish centuries of darkness?* Victory for him was turning in his homework on time. Sailing through a cursed sea to attack a towering stone fortress on a zombie-infested island was a little bit out of his league.

"It is the second sign we have received," Zaputo continued. "The second sign that the hardships we have endured are finally drawing to a close."

"What was the first sign?" Willa asked.

"The fire bird."

"The what?"

Zaputo stroked the chest of the bird riding on his shoulder. "We feared the fire bird was extinct, but it appeared just before dawn. Legend tells us that when a fiery red bird returned to the leader of Aquat, our people would rise again."

Tom nodded impatiently. That was all fine, but they were getting off topic. He backed it up a step and asked, "Can the *Crimson Belle* get us through the Coral Canyon, and then all the way to the southern harbor of Arx?"

Zaputo puffed up his chest. "The *Crimson Belle* can sail anything."

Tom nodded. Okay. That was a start. Now they just had to deal with hundreds of rabid, disgusting, flesh-eating scavengers. He looked at Porter.

His brother chewed his lower lip as he studied the map. Then he drew his finger from their destination, the fortress on the northern end of the island, to the rocky beach which lay to the south. "How close can we get to the beach?"

"A few hundred yards away," Zaputo said. "Any closer and we risk running aground."

Porter nodded. "Will your cannon reach that far? Maybe we can blast our way through the scavengers before we go inland."

"That won't work," Willa said. "No cannon, arrows, clubs, or swords. The only way to drive them back is with flame."

That meant a full frontal assault—rowing ashore, then getting close enough to the creatures to thrust a torch in whatever was left of their stinking, slimy faces. Not exactly an exciting prospect. And even if they took nearly all of Zaputo's crew with them, they still didn't have enough manpower to stand a chance. They'd immediately be swarmed.

Porter must have come to the same conclusion, for his face fell. "There aren't enough of us," he said. "We need twice as many men and twice as many boats to take on the scavengers."

Twice as many men . . .

As Porter's words echoed through his mind, Tom felt the tension that had bubbled up inside him suddenly shift, like popping the cap on a bottle of soda. "Exactly," he murmured, his mind racing. He looked at Porter. "You're right. That's exactly what we need. Twice as many men and twice as many boats."

"Why do you sound like that's a good thing?"

"Umbrey! He's still out there—I know he is. He wouldn't have left us. All we have to do is signal for his help."

Willa's eyes flew open wide. "You're right."

Mudge whirled around to face Zaputo. "Do you have a Mayday flag?"

A look of sour distaste showed on Zaputo's face. "You ask the *Crimson Belle* to fly the flag of a ship in extreme distress? A flag of weakness?"

"The flag of a ship that requires immediate assistance," Mudge corrected.

Zaputo let out a harsh breath. He considered the request for a moment, then gave a reluctant nod to one of his crewman. The man conveyed the order and within a matter of minutes the colors had been raised. From the rear mast fluttered a crisp white flag with a bold blue cross in the center.

"A waste of time," Zaputo said. "This captain, this Umbrey of yours, will not come. If he has any brains at all, he'll assume it's a trick."

Mudge shook his head. He lightly ran his fingers along the hilt of the Sword of Five Kingdoms, which he now carried tucked in his belt, in the same fashion as Zaputo carried his own weapon. "You'll see," he said. "The people of Divino have learned from their mistakes. This time the Mayday flag will be answered."

They stood together against the rail, scanning the horizon. Tom clenched his fists and rapped his knuckles impatiently against his thigh. Waiting. Sharp slivers of doubt pierced his thoughts as time ticked slowly past. Where was Umbrey? What if they were wrong? What if Umbrey had left them? What if he was simply too far away to see the flag? What if—

The *Purgatory* coasted into view, her crisp white sails billowing against the brilliant morning sky. Umbrey.

Tom let out a long, deep breath. Beside him, Porter slammed his fist in victory against the ship's rail, and Willa gave a wild cheer. A beaming smile broke out across Mudge's face.

"I *knew* it," Mudge said. "I knew he'd come."

Zaputo's crew launched into action, lowering the *Crimson Belle's* sails and bringing her into alignment with the *Purgatory*. Within a matter of minutes the two ships were so close they were almost touching. Umbrey's crew tossed ropes to Zaputo's men, who caught them and began tugging, drawing the *Purgatory* closer, inch by inch, until the two hulls gently bumped and the ropes were tied off. As a last measure, a broad wooden plank was put in place between them, allowing the crew to traverse from one ship to the other.

The next sound Tom heard was the steady *thunk* of Umbrey's peg leg as he walked, alone, across the plank. He reached the end and stopped. Fisting his hands on his hips, he frowned as he looked at Tom, Porter, Willa, and Mudge.

"Well, you're alive," he said. "At least there's that. But I've seen you look better."

Tom glanced at his friends. It wasn't pretty. Porter's face was bruised, a cut scabbing over his left eye, and his clothing was torn. Willa's hair was mussed, her face and clothing little better than Porter's. Mudge looked equally battle worn, and Tom knew his own appearance was just as bad. His lower lip was split, and was so swollen it felt like he'd kissed a pufferfish.

"Rough morning," he said.

"So I gather." Umbrey looked at Zaputo. "You're responsible for that?"

Zaputo locked his arms over his broad chest and scowled. "They attempted to organize a mutiny among the captives. My men defended this ship, as they are trained to do."

Umbrey nodded, considering the other man's words. He gestured toward Tom, Porter, Willa, and Mudge. "But you let them live anyway."

Zaputo gave an indifferent shrug. "For the moment."

Umbrey stepped off the plank and moved to stand before Zaputo. The fiery bird perched on Zaputo's shoulder emitted a sharp *caw!* and ruffled its feathers as the two men silently sized each other up. Umbrey must not have minded what he saw, for he extended his hand.

"Umbrey," he said, by way of introduction. "Captain of the *Purgatory*."

Zaputo grudgingly shook his proffered hand. "Salvador Zaputo. Captain of the *Crimson Belle* and ruler of Aquat."

"I saw your flag," Umbrey continued. His gaze moved across the deck. "But I see no signs of distress."

Zaputo tilted his head toward Tom and his friends. "I will let them speak," Zaputo said. "They are good at that. Especially the little one."

Willa and Mudge stepped forward. Together, the two of them outlined their plan. After a brief discussion, Umbrey gave his assent to take the dinghies from the *Purgatory* onto the *Crimson Belle*. Once they were properly transferred and lashed to the side, Umbrey mounted a wooden box and addressed his crew.

"Men of the *Purgatory*," he bellowed, "we have answered a Mayday call. The *Crimson Belle* needs our assistance. They will be sailing into the Cursed Souls Sea. They require able-bodied men to join them in their fight to rid our lands of scavengers. A few of you will have to stay behind to defend the *Purgatory*, but for the rest of you there is no guarantee you'll return alive, or that you'll return at all." He paused, a scowl on his face as he scratched the stubble on his chin. "Most likely you'll be torn to bits by flesh-eating scavengers, be devoured by sharks, starve to death on some godforsaken island, or die some other gruesome death too horrible and painful to name."

Tom shook his head. Nothing like sticking to the pure, unvarnished truth to really motivate people.

Umbrey slapped his hands together and rubbed them briskly. "On the other hand, you might just succeed in ridding our lands of those vile creatures once and for all. So. There you have it. You've been told what you're up against. Who among you will risk his life to help them?"

His crew gave a roar and surged across the plank, joining the men of the *Crimson Belle*. Umbrey nodded approvingly. "They're a rough, scurvy lot, but they've got spine." Then he stepped down from his makeshift podium and looked at Zaputo. "They're well trained, as loyal as the day is long, and they follow orders. You'll get no trouble from them."

They wasted no time getting to work. There was much to do, and little time to do it. A few of the Divino captives—very young children and infants, along with the elderly or those too ill to fight—were escorted back to the *Purgatory*. The rest of the men and women of Divino remained aboard the *Crimson Belle* to assist with the coming battle at Arx.

They transferred dinghies from one ship to the other and lashed them to the side. The *Crimson Belle* lost her sleek lines, but the boats would be necessary for them to get everyone ashore.

Next they fashioned club-like torches for weapons. Using brooms, mops, oars, or any other piece of wood they could get their hands on, they wrapped one end in heavy canvas and soaked it in kerosene, creating what looked to Tom like dozens of enormous matches. Last of all, they primed and loaded their cannons.

As they worked, Zaputo's bird perched itself on the deck rail, its beady eyes watching the proceedings with an intensity that was unnerving for a creature that wasn't human.

"Is it just me, or is that bird kind of creepy?" Tom said to Porter, pausing between the tasks of finishing the torches and loading them on the boats.

Porter wiped the sweat from his brow and shrugged. "It's a bird."

"I know that. But there's something about it." Something he hadn't liked the moment he set eyes on the thing. Not only had his dislike been instant, but it had been tinged with recognition. There was a reason he didn't like it. He'd seen it somewhere before. "I mean, doesn't it look familiar to you?"

"No."

Tom sighed. There was something about that bird...

As if reading his thoughts, the bird turned its beady eyes on

Tom. With a single beat of its wings, it soared straight toward him. Tom gave a yelp and hit the deck. The bird's razor-sharp beak missed his eye by mere inches.

Porter smirked and looked at him. "If I were you, I'd forget about the bird, and get back to work."

Tom rose shakily, looking for the bird. It was perched far above the deck, on the crow's nest. Forcing himself to ignore it, he returned his attention to his work. It was almost time to go.

Zaputo strode to the quarterdeck and surveyed the sea of faces below him. "If any man or woman wishes to leave this vessel, do so now."

No one moved.

Zaputo gave a satisfied nod. "No ship has ever lasted the night in the Cursed Souls Sea," he said. "We will return before the sun sets."

Or not at all, Tom thought.

Umbrey nodded. Satisfied he'd done as much as he could to help, he turned to go.

Tom stared at him in shocked disbelief. "You're not coming with us?"

"Me? No, lad. Not this trip. A ship only has room for one captain at a time."

He crossed the plank to the *Purgatory* and threw off the lines that bound the ships together. Using his good foot, he kicked the plank into the water. A swarm of greedy undertoads, apparently mistaking it for food, issued high-pitched squeals of delight. They grabbed the plank with their skinny suction cup fingers and dragged it underwater.

"Safe voyage!" Umbrey called as he began to drift away. "Keep your wits about you and bring back that blasted book!"

CHAPTER FIFTEEN

CORAL CANYON

"Eat now. The water will be too rough to balance a plate once we enter the Cursed Souls Sea."

Tom turned in surprise to see Porter standing behind him, offering a plate of food. He took it with a word of thanks and lifted the fork. It wasn't as good as the food Umbrey served—this meal consisted of some kind of fish stew and spicy rice—but it was plentiful and filling and Tom was glad to have it. He scraped the plate clean, then washed it down with a tankard of cool cider.

To his surprise, Porter hadn't walked away after delivering the food. Instead, his brother sat down beside him as he ate and stared across the horizon. Although Porter's posture was relaxed, Tom knew him well enough to recognize the subtle tension that ran through him. Sensing he had something on his mind, he waited for Porter to break the silence that hung between them.

"You get any sleep?" Porter finally asked.

Tom shrugged. "Yeah, some." After last night, he'd badly needed it. He'd allowed himself to drift off shortly after the *Crimson Belle* had gotten under way. As it was now midday, he guessed he'd slept for four hours or so. He glanced at his brother, noting the dark smudges beneath his eyes. "You?"

"A little." Porter heaved a sigh and dragged his fingers through his pale blond hair. "Why'd you do it?"

"Do what?"

"Tell Zaputo that the attack on his men was all your idea. Put your neck on the line like that. I wouldn't have done it for you."

"Thanks, guy."

Porter laughed. "I didn't mean it like that. I just meant . . ." His voice drifted away for a moment. Then he gathered himself and said, "I don't know. Maybe I did. I mean, it worked, but what were you thinking?"

"Thinking?" Tom repeated. "I wasn't thinking at all. I just . . . did it. It just seems like every minute that passes where we aren't dead is a good thing."

Porter gave him a long, hard look. "So that's it? That's your strategy? Just do whatever it takes to stay alive one more minute?"

"Yeah. Pretty much."

"And that works for you?"

"Look, we made it, didn't we? We're still here. So I guess everything worked out okay."

"Maybe for now." Porter shifted, stretching his legs out in front of him. Tom could almost feel the agitation coursing through him. "But what happens when it doesn't work out?"

"What do you mean? You think things might go wrong?"

Porter regarded him as though he were an idiot. "When has anything we've ever done *not* gone wrong?"

Excellent point.

"Okay. So you're worried about what'll happen when we get to Arx."

"Right. But not just that. This is my *home*. It's all I have." Porter shook his head, obviously working himself up to what he really wanted to say. His gaze locked on Tom. "You don't care, because you don't have to. You come here, pull all these ridiculous stunts and act like some kind of hero. If things don't work out, you can just shrug it off and leave. I don't have that option."

Tom looked at his brother. For a second, he thought he was joking. Then he realized Porter was completely serious. Tom suddenly understood why the only time he felt connected to him was when they were bringing maps to life. The rest of the time he just didn't understand him. Didn't *want* to understand him.

"So that's your way of saying thanks, huh?"

"Thanks?" A muscle twitched in Porter's jaw. "You've been lucky, I'll give you that. But you've got to stop pushing it. One of these times your luck's going to run out. You're going to try to play hero and end up killing somebody. I don't want to be around when that happens."

Tom let out a low breath, battling an urge to shove his fist in his brother's face. "You want to keep score, fine. Let's go back to your carefully thought-out plan to take on Zaputo's crew. Real smart thinking. How'd that work out for you?"

Porter's pale eyes darkened. He opened his mouth, then seemed to change his mind. "What I'm trying to say," he began, his voice low and controlled, "is that we need a plan. If we try to just figure things out when we get to Arx we won't make it out alive."

Tom removed the map of the Cursed Souls Sea from his inner coat pocket and spread it open. He pointed to the island of Arx. "Look. The *Crimson Belle* lands in the southern harbor and we all row ashore, battle the scavengers, and somehow manage to live long enough to actually make it across the island and into the fortress, where we grab the Black Book of Pernicus."

"Right."

"Then what?"

Tom blinked. As he looked at the map, Porter's meaning suddenly became clear. They hadn't come up with an escape strategy yet.

Their plan to get ashore was a blunt one. The assembled group of captives and crewmen would divert the scavengers with a noisy battle on the southern end of the island, allowing Tom, Porter, Willa, and Mudge time to sneak past the scavengers and race to the northern fortress. A clear path and a running start—that was the best they could hope for.

But no one thought the battle could go on indefinitely. There were just too many scavengers. At some point, the captives and crew would have to retreat back to the relative safety of the *Crimson Belle*.

Which meant that once Tom and his friends made it past the beach, they were on their own.

So how were they supposed to get *back* to the ship? They couldn't return the way they came—not by themselves, when the landing beach would be swarming with scavengers. Obviously their best bet would be to grab the book and leave directly from the fortress. But how? Even if the *Crimson Belle* came around to wait for them off the northern end of the island, how were they supposed to get back to the ship from a towering fortress perched on a cliff? Jump and swim for it? The fall alone would probably kill them.

"I see what you mean," Tom said. "I guess I haven't figured it out quite yet."

"Well, you let me know when you do. If we could fly, we might stand a chance. But since that's not going to happen, we need a plan."

As if listening to their conversation, Zaputo's bird left its perch on the crow's nest and soared past their heads, gliding over the sea in tighter and tighter circles until it dove into the water and snatched an enormous fish in its talons. It dropped the flopping fish on the deck with an ugly *splat!* then proceeded to make a meal of it, tearing the fish apart with its beak.

"We've got to bring ropes," Porter continued. "Once we grab the book, we'll scale down the tower to the rocks at the base of the cliff. From there, Zaputo can send his crewmen with a boat to pick us up. I've been thinking about it for a while now. That's our only way back to the *Crimson Belle*."

Tom mulled over Porter's plan. In theory, it *might* work. Except for one thing. He glanced at the map. Unlike the relatively calm southern shore, the waves at the northern tip of the island violently crashed against the fortress cliff.

"The sea is pretty rough there, isn't it?" he said.

"I'd rather take my chances against the sea than a beach full of scavengers."

"Right." Tom nodded. He thought for a long moment, but couldn't come up with a better solution. "If only we could fly," he said absently, his gaze landing on the fiery bird. Moving with vicious efficiency, it had torn off the fish's flesh, spread its guts across the deck and pecked apart its bones.

"Yeah. But I don't think even you can pull that off."

As Tom watched the bird devouring its meal, Zaputo stuck two fingers in his mouth and emitted an ear-splitting whistle. The bird gave a sharp caw and tore off the fish's head. Grasping it in its talons, it flew to the captain. Zaputo gave the bird an approving pat, then sucked on the slimy fish head, smacking his lips in satisfaction.

Tom's stomach turned. Disgusting.

Willa and Mudge approached. "Look," Willa said, indicating a shimmering spot in the distance. "The Coral Canyon. We're almost there."

Already? Tom thought, battling a sudden bout of nerves. Keegan had allotted them only three days to retrieve the Black Book of Pernicus and return it to him. Tom knew they had to move fast. He *wanted* to move fast. But that didn't make the prospect of landing on a scavenger-infested island any less terrifying—particularly if they didn't have a firm plan in place to get off that same island.

He rose and moved to the ship's rail. Porter tucked the map away and joined him. Together the four watched in fascinated silence as the *Crimson Belle* sailed toward the canyon. From a distance, it looked like nothing more than a glowing pink blur on the horizon. But as they drew closer, Tom was able to make out a series of jagged peaks jutting up out of the sea.

He had assumed the *Crimson Belle* would merely have to make its way through a single, hourglass-shaped gap in the canyon. Difficult, but not necessarily deadly. What he saw before him, however, made his throat draw tight with fear.

The passage to the Cursed Souls Sea was far more treacherous than anything he could have imagined. The canyon wasn't actually a canyon at all. It was an obstacle course, filled with razor-sharp columns of glittery pink coral that shot up at random intervals, thrusting out of the sea like a series of spiky stalagmites. The ship would have to slalom its way through them to get to the other side, fighting against wind and currents which threatened to drive them into the coral and shred the hull.

If they'd been in a car, Tom would have wanted to slam on the brakes and turn around. But obviously that wasn't an option.

Ignoring the fluttering drum roll in his belly, his gaze returned to Salvador Zaputo. The captain had moved to the foredeck beside the ship's pilot. He lowered the spyglass he held, seemed to think for a moment, then calmly conveyed an order to his crew.

If he was at all intimidated by the task of safely navigating his ship through the perilous canyon, his face didn't show it. He looked cool and collected, completely in command.

Tom swallowed hard and tried to draw some comfort from that. He noted Willa's white-knuckled grip on the ship's rail. "We'll make it," he said to her. "If Zaputo's not worried, we shouldn't be."

Willa let out a shallow breath. "Right," she said, forcing a shaky smile. But Tom noticed her grip didn't lessen any.

Zaputo's men furled the mainsails, leaving nothing but the topsails fluttering. They paused for a moment just outside the entrance to the Coral Canyon. The ship stalled, as though caught between shifting currents. Or perhaps giving them time to reconsider their decision to enter the canyon. Up close, the coral glittered like thousands of shards of broken glass, just waiting to rip them to pieces.

Despite the reassurances he'd offered Willa, Tom found he couldn't calm his own nerves. His stomach performed a series of somersaults and his heart fluttered in his chest. The *Crimson Belle* shuddered and groaned as though issuing a final protest, or maybe a warning of imminent danger ahead, just the way the *Purgatory* had before it plunged over the edge of the earth.

All around him, Tom could feel the passengers and crew of the *Crimson Belle* catching their breath and holding it. Waiting. Porter clutched the map in his fist and shifted anxiously. Mudge locked his palm around the hilt of the Sword of Five Kingdoms, which remained tucked at his side. The boy chewed his lower lip. He opened his mouth as if to speak, but his words died in his throat. No one dared break the tense silence that surrounded them.

The moment stretched out. Then, like a roller coaster reaching the crest of a hill, the ship's bow drifted into place and the ship launched.

They shot forward, propelled by winds and currents and gravitational forces Tom couldn't begin to define. Had Zaputo not been the captain he was, or his crew so highly trained, the *Crimson Belle* would have splintered into pieces many times over. Instead they repeatedly came within a hair's breadth of collision with the jagged coral peaks, only to veer away from utter disaster with just seconds to spare.

Then, just when Tom was certain their luck would finally run out, they passed their last obstacle. They'd made it through. But any elation he might have felt at still being alive withered and died as he looked at what awaited them.

The Cursed Souls Sea.

The sky was bile green, thick with whirling gray clouds that twisted around and around like the eye of a tornado. Water spouts and towering waves sprang up from a churning sea that frothed and foamed in violent shades of purple and black. Within the waves Tom caught glimpses of scaly, gargantuan creatures that looked like squid—only unlike the squid he was used to seeing, these were armed with enormous fangs. Other sea monsters lurked just below the waterline, but Tom couldn't see those as clearly. He could only make out a sinister, slithering impression of the slippery beasts.

That alone was terrifying. But worst of all was the wind. It seemed to come at them from all sides, howling and screeching as it whipped across the deck. It wasn't a normal wind at all. This sounded like demonic laughter, as though Pernicus himself was marking their approach and shrieking with delight.

As though he'd been eagerly expecting them.

As though the *ship*, and all those aboard it, was heading right into his trap. They sailed headlong into the Cursed Souls Sea.

CHAPTER SIXTEEN

The *Crimson Belle* pitched and rolled, carried by swiftly moving currents that were beyond even Zaputo's control. A few pockets of the sea were as dark and slick as blackened sheets of ice. Other stretches churned with violently twisting whirlpools that sucked everything that came near them into their deadly wake. They scooted past those dangers, only to be drawn up into towering waves that shot them skyward, then sent them plummeting down the opposite side.

Willa let out a soft groan and lowered her head. Tom gave her a sideways glance. Although she remained standing, she was deathly pale and her skin had a delicate green hue. Seasick, he guessed.

He nodded toward her satchel. "You have any herbs in there that could help your stomach?" he asked.

"Probably, I would have taken something, but I guess I didn't think it would be this bad."

"We're almost there," he said, hoping to reassure her, though in truth he had no idea where they were.

She let out a long, uneven breath. "You think so?"

"Definitely." At least he hoped so. They didn't have time to drift about aimlessly. Not if they wanted to make it out of the Cursed Souls Sea and back through the Coral Canyon before nightfall.

He started to say more, but his attention was captured by a tiny spec that appeared on the horizon. Tom squinted, watching the spec grow larger and larger until he was able to identify the object as a ship—a ship that traveled in the opposite direction they were moving.

He tensed, momentarily convinced that Keegan had decided he didn't need them after all. That his men had somehow made it to Arx, and were now on their way back to Divino with the Black Book of Pernicus.

But what he saw was much, much worse.

The passengers and crew of the *Crimson Belle* lined the rails to watch in horror as the vessel drifted past. The ship's sails had been ripped to shreds, its lines were tangled, its deck was rough and worn. There was no evidence of anyone onboard—or rather, no evidence of any *living* being onboard.

The ship had been seized by scavengers.

They hung from the masts and staggered across the decks. Seaweed-drenched scavengers clung to the hull. They peered out through the portholes and swung from the crow's nest, their rotted, mangled bodies filling every inch of the ship.

Once the *Crimson Belle* was spotted, a fevered cry went up among the creatures. They moaned and writhed in frenzied excitement, hunching up and down, their arms stretched out as though to pluck the *Crimson Belle's* passengers off the deck and greedily devour them right where they stood.

Fortunately, the ships were too far apart for that to be possible, though more than a few scavengers toppled into the sea attempting it. An octopus-like arm shot up from the murky depths, wrapped around the flailing scavengers, and pulled them under. A few seconds later a greasy stain bubbled to the surface.

Tom shuddered. The scavenger's ship continued past, becoming smaller and smaller as it drifted into the distance. Off to terrorize the people of Aquat, Divino, or some other land? he wondered. Tom tore his gaze away, looking for something else to focus on, when one of Zaputo's crewmen bellowed a single word.

"Land!"

Tom spun around. His eyes locked on a rocky, terracotta -colored island shimmering on the horizon.

Zaputo stepped forward. He peered into the distance. A triumphant glimmer entered his dark eyes. He sucked in a deep gulp of air, then breathed out a single word.

"Arx."

They'd made it.

As the *Crimson Belle* drew closer, Tom shielded his eyes and was able to make out the skeletal remains of the island city. He saw towering buildings, coliseums, fountains, three-story pillars framing an outdoor stage, enormous statues—all carved from the same shimmering pink stone.

The site reminded him of sketches he'd seen of ancient Rome. The structures were badly decayed, huge swaths of stone now broken and crumbling to dust, but enough remained for him to imagine how spectacular the city must once have been.

After a moment, Zaputo seemed to shake himself out of the stupor into which he'd fallen. "Bring her about and prepare to anchor!" he shouted.

His crew sprang into action. Aided by the men of the *Purgatory*, they trimmed the sails and, after a brief struggle with the prevailing winds and currents, succeeded in bringing the *Crimson Belle* about. That accomplished, they went directly to work positioning the cannon, unlashing the dinghies, and readying the boats for launch.

Porter and Mudge came to stand beside Tom and Willa at the ship's rail. From a distance, the harbor of Arx looked idyllic—a shallow, crescent shaped bay filled with shimmering turquoise water which gently lapped against a pristine white beach. A honeymooner's paradise.

Up close, however, the harbor told a different story. Tom peered into the water brushing the hull. It was thick with barbed fish, fanged eels, spiny crab, and oozing octopi. Borrowing a nearby spyglass to get a closer look, he scanned the shoreline where their boats would land. The white surface wasn't sand at all, he noted, but the remains of crushed bones and skulls that had washed up against the shore. All that was left of those who'd tried to take the island before them.

He lowered the spyglass and passed it to Porter, watching as his brother scanned the shore. Porter didn't say a word, but as he set the spyglass aside, Tom noted that his expression had tightened into one of grim understanding.

"Ready to fire!" shouted a crewman, standing by a primed and loaded cannon.

Fast. It was happening fast. Obviously Zaputo was as mindful as Tom was of the need for urgency. Or perhaps he simply didn't want to give anyone time to give in to the terror that was gripping them and retreat before the battle had even begun.

Zaputo gave a signal, and his men touched their torches to the fuses. Five cannon roared simultaneously, belching smoke and gunpowder as they hurled cannonballs over the water to crash against the rocky shoreline. Zaputo's men loaded and fired again. Then again.

While the cannon fire wouldn't kill the scavengers outright (at most they might knock off a limb or two), with any luck the noise would serve to lure the creatures out of their hiding spots and draw them down to the shore.

Their goal was to gather all the scavengers at the southern end of the island and pin them there long enough for Tom, Porter, Willa, and Mudge to slip unnoticed through the chaos on the beach and dash to the fortress in the north.

The cannon fire seemed to be working. As Tom watched, dozens of scavengers drawn to the noise and commotion, staggered out from behind piles of rubble and climbed over broken ruins. They stumbled to the shore, their peeling flesh quivering with excitement, filling the air with their hideous grunts and moans. The wind lifted the scent of their rotting bodies and carried it to the *Crimson Belle*. Tom took a deep breath, held it in, and turned away, willing himself not to breathe it in.

"Launch the boats!" ordered Zaputo.

Time to go ashore. They crowded the dinghies with the former captives from Divino, the crew from the *Purgatory*, and the men of the *Crimson Belle*. After ensuring that each man and woman aboard received a flaming torch, the boats were dropped into the water. At least a dozen boats strong, they formed a fiery flotilla around the hull of the *Crimson Belle*.

Tom gripped a torch and seated himself between Willa and Mudge in the last boat. His heart drummed painfully against his ribs. The roar of his pulse pounding in his ears was so loud it nearly blocked out the frenzied groans of the scavengers. But not quite. He shot a glance at Porter, seeing the same strain reflected on his brother's face.

The conversation they'd had earlier replayed itself in his mind. Porter was right. What they were about to do now, getting from the ship to the island, would be difficult. But the reverse, getting off the island and back onto the *Crimson Belle*, would be almost impossible. Even with the thick coils of rope they each wore slung sideways across their chest—rope they hoped would help them scale down the side of the tower and escape — returning to the *Crimson Belle* would be a miracle.

He glanced up. The sun had past its zenith and was beginning its descent. They wouldn't have long on the island. Less than an hour, certainly. He wasn't even sure they'd last that long.

He had to think of something. They'd already fixed their current plan with Zaputo, but they needed a better one. A faster way off the island and back to the ship. But what?

His eyes darted around the ship for something—*anything*— that might spark an idea. Yards and yards of rope, heavy brass cleats used to secure the lines, acres of canvas, oars, fine netting, barrels of water, wooden cases of provisions, cloth and thread . . . swords, knives, axes . . . pots, pans, trays . . . plenty there if he could just *think*.

Zaputo gave a final command to his crew—a handful of men were to remain aboard to ready the ship for departure and prevent any scavengers from sneaking on—and moved to join them in the last boat. As he stepped toward them, Zaputo's bird ruffled his wings, fluttered in the air for a second or two, then resettled itself on the captain's shoulder.

"Wait!" Tom shouted. He lurched to his feet, causing the boat to rock precariously. The other passengers gasped, glaring at him as they steadied the vessel. Oblivious to the disaster he'd almost caused, he looked at Porter. "Listen. You said the only way to make it out of the fortress and back to the ship was if we could fly."

Porter scowled at him. "What are you talking about?"

"We can't fly. But Zaupto's bird can."

"I still don't—"

"I've got an idea. Hold this!"

Tom thrust his torch at his brother. He leapt off the boat and back onto the deck of the *Crimson Belle*. After a brief discussion with Zaputo, he reached for the pile of spare cleats. The cleats were made of heavy brass, roughly the shape and size of a shallow boomerang, with thick knobs on both ends. Traditionally, a cleat was bolted to the deck and a rope twisted around it in a figure-eight, thus securing the line.

But Tom had in mind a very different use for them. He grabbed four of the largest and most highly polished cleats he could find, and climbed back into the boat.

"What are those?" Mudge asked.

"Plan B," he answered. "Just in case." He looked at Willa. "Here. Give me your satchel." He thrust the heavy cleats into the satchel, then draped the bag diagonally across his chest, carrying it alongside the coiled rope.

A moment later Zaputo stepped into the boat, his weight causing the vessel to tilt slightly toward the stern. Zaputo's dark gaze silently swept over the flotilla. Tom caught his breath, as did everyone around him. Seconds passed. All eyes locked on the captain of the *Crimson Belle*.

Zaputo raised his torch.

"*Attack!*" he roared.

An ear-splitting chorus of cheers and yells answered him. Within each boat, a single crewman lifted his oars and began pulling toward shore. The passengers gripped their torches and readied themselves for battle. As they neared Arx, waves caught their boats and carried them inland.

But even with the tide at their backs, they didn't make it.

The scavengers swarmed their boats before they touched shore.

CHAPTER SEVENTEEN

IMPOSSIBLE TOWER

The creatures staggered into the waves, lunging toward them. It happened too fast for Tom to properly sort it out. One second they were coasting toward the shore, the next second the scavengers were swarming their boats, nearly tipping them over in a rabid desperation to reach their prey.

As he clambered out of his boat, Tom struck out with his torch, forcing the scavengers back. He was dimly aware of Porter and Willa tumbling out of the boat beside him, of the water lapping his thighs and the current threatening to pull him under, of Mudge knocked under the waves and then struggling back to the surface, of Zaputo using his feet to kick the hollow-chested, hissing scavengers away.

There was no structured fight. Just brutal, ugly chaos. The twisted, furious faces of the scavengers. Their claw-like hands and gaping mouths, their torn flesh and shredded clothing, the stench of their rotting bodies. Flailing torches, crashing waves, overturned boats. Everywhere he looked, the same horror presented itself.

Mudge's tumble in the water, had extinguished his torch, leaving him defenseless. A second later, a scavenger caught

Willa by the ankle and pulled her under. Her torch hit the water with a fiery hiss, then went out. Porter knocked the scavenger clear and pulled Willa, drenched and gasping, back to her feet.

It wasn't going well. Barely a minute into the battle, and they'd already lost half their weapons. For a moment, the attack teetered on the verge of disaster, over before it had even begun.

But despite the rough beginning, Zaputo and his men succeeded in driving the scavengers back, pushing them away from the boats. Somehow they made it to the shore. They couldn't hold out for long, however. Even with the combined forces of the *Crimson Belle*, the *Purgatory*, and the captives from Divino, there were simply too many of the wretched creatures to keep at bay.

So caught up was he in the battle, Tom had to remind himself why they were there. They didn't come to Arx to fight the scavengers, but to get the book. If he held out any hope at all of doing that, they needed to get to the fortress *now*.

Porter had apparently reached the same conclusion. As Tom swung his torch, knocking a particularly nasty gray-haired scavenger to his knees, he felt his brother give his shoulder a rough shove.

"Go!" Porter shouted. "*Now!*"

Zaputo and four of his men moved into place to shield them from the battle. Tom, with Porter, Willa, and Mudge beside him, took off at a sprint, stumbling over shattered skulls and bones, dimly aware of the horrific scene he was leaving behind.

They raced away from the beach and found a crude trail that appeared to lead north. The path led them across the ruins of Arx. They sped past collapsed columns and crumbling amphitheaters, ducked under fallen edifices and leapt over piles of broken rubble. All around them were the badly deteriorating remains of the ancient city. An archaeologist's dream—or

nightmare, depending on one's point of view. All Tom knew for certain was that they had to keep moving.

His lungs burned and a deep cramp pierced his side. Tom lost track of how long they'd been running or how much land they'd covered when he heard Willa shout.

"Look!"

Breathing hard, he staggered to a stop and turned his gaze in the direction she pointed. Although he hadn't been fully conscious of it, he noted now that the path they'd been following had taken them uphill. They stood on a rocky, coastal bluff overlooking the harbor.

The flotilla of boats they'd taken ashore was heading back to the *Crimson Belle*. There was no mistaking what that meant. Zaputo and the others had held off the scavengers for as long as they could. Now Tom, Porter, Willa, and Mudge were on their own. Just the four of them alone on the island. Just the four of them . . . and whatever revolting, undead creatures lurked among the rubble.

Tom swallowed hard as fear knotted his stomach. He dragged in a deep breath, then nodded to the fortress. "It's all right," he said. "We're almost there."

He took a second to survey their surroundings. The dominant feature, of course, was the tower fortress, which loomed directly ahead of them. Cylindrical in shape and built of dark, uneven stone, it sat perched on the edge of a cliff overlooking the sea. Something about the structure struck him as medieval in design, and vaguely sinister—the sort of place where a king might be locked up before his beheading.

The rest of their surroundings had the washed-out, pale look of desert terrain that had baked in the sun for centuries. Or maybe a lunar landscape was a better way to describe it. There were no trees, no bushes, no scrubs or grasses. No water anywhere. The ruins of the ancient city were long behind them. Now all Tom could see were craters, boulders, and rocks. Everything was dry and dusty.

The trail they followed hooked slightly to the left, curving up toward the fortress. Initially, the path had struck Tom as a poor imitation of a road. At this juncture, however, it revealed itself to be what it truly was: a loose scrabble of rocks and gravel that flowed uphill.

He turned his attention back to the tower. But the longer he looked at it, the more convinced he was they shouldn't go anywhere near it. Some deep, inner alarm sounded a warning to stay away. Far away. He ignored it. They didn't have a choice.

"C'mon," he said, "let's get this over with."

They clawed their way up the path, hunching down low to use their hands, as well as their feet, where the ground rose too steeply to be traversed any other way. The late afternoon sun beat down mercilessly, causing Tom's hands to grow slick with sweat. A dry howling wind kicked up, but it did little to cool him off. His head was pounding, his lips were parched, and a fine dust coated his throat, making it almost impossible to swallow. Water. They should have brought water.

It doesn't matter, he told himself. *They were almost there. They had to be. Just one more turn around the bend...*

But with every turn, circling the structure over and over, the tower never seemed to get any closer.

Tom drew to a sudden stop. "Wait," he said, his voice little more than a hoarse croak. They should have been there by now. Something was wrong. It shouldn't be taking this long.

He looked at Porter, Willa, and Mudge. They were sweaty, coated with dust, so exhausted they swayed on their feet. The dried saltwater had stiffened their clothing, and the rope they each carried slung across their chests had rubbed raw sores into the sides of their necks. In addition, Tom and Porter had both been carrying torches. Tom's arm ached, his muscles trembling with the strain of keeping the torch aloft.

They'd been climbing for what felt like hours, yet they were no closer to the tower. It didn't make sense.

The wind picked up again, but this time Tom heard something within it that he'd been too exhausted, too focused on his climb, to hear before.

Pernicus's laughter.

It was a trick. There was no way to reach the tower. At least, not the way they were attempting it. Porter and Willa must have heard it as well, for Porter let out a black oath, while Willa sank down on a boulder, her expression utterly defeated.

"We'll never make it," she said.

Tom shot a glance at the horizon. The last time he'd checked, the sun was overhead. Now the fiery orange ball looked nearly ready to sink into the Cursed Souls Sea.

"We have to keep climbing," Mudge said. "We can't just give up."

"We're out of time," Porter spat out, looking both furious and overwhelmed.

Not yet. Tom studied the distant tower. They *had* to get there. How?

"What if we—" he began, but Willa cut him off.

"Shhh!" she said, her face suddenly tense. "Did you hear

145

that?"

Tom listened. Wind. Waves crashing against the rocks below. The caw of a bird flying overhead. Nothing. He lifted his shoulders in an indifferent shrug, then abruptly froze.

This time he heard it. A sound that was impossible to mistake for anything else. A dull, monotone groan that made the hairs on the back of his neck stand at attention. The sound repeated over and over, growing louder as it moved toward them.

Scavengers.

His head snapped up. They'd wasted so much time circling the tower, they'd given the scavengers time to catch them.

He watched in helpless terror as the scavengers appeared, stumbling toward them. They climbed over rocks and boulders, staggering forward with their arms outstretched, their bulging eyes glittering with hunger and rage. Within seconds they surrounded the four of them on all sides, at least a dozen strong, maybe more.

Moving slowly, cautiously, Tom formed a tight circle with Porter, Willa, and Mudge, their shoulders touching as they faced outward.

Tom brought up his torch and his heart stopped. The oil-soaked canvas, bright and blazing when he'd left the *Crimson Belle*, had dwindled down to a sputtering flame. He'd been so focused on reaching the tower he hadn't noticed that his torch was dying. He cut a glance at Porter's weapon, only to find that his brother faced the same predicament.

As though sensing their advantage, the creatures issued excited grunts and shoved past each other in their frenzy to reach the foursome. Tom felt sharp yellow claws tug at his clothing. Using his torch as a club, he swung wildly, attempting to beat them back. But there were too many. With every inch of space he gained, more scavengers appeared to crowd them in.

He heard the fury in Porter's voice as he screamed at the creatures to back off, the terror and desperation in Willa's. It was a losing battle and they all knew it. There was nothing they could do, no way to hold the creatures at bay, no matter how much they might wish—

Wish.

Tom's thoughts skidded to a stop. The folly's rattle.

He dug into his pocket and yanked it free. The rattle warmed his palm, throbbing as rapidly as his own heartbeat and emitting a bright pinkish-orange glow.

There was no time to think. No time to plan a proper strategy or worry about exact wording. Not if they wanted to survive.

"Save us from these scavengers!" he yelled.

For a moment, nothing happened. Then the earth beneath his feet began to tremble. Softly at first, then with increasing fury, until the entire cliff was shaking. An ear-splitting *crack* reverberated through the air. The hill upon which they stood crested like a wave, then came crashing down.

A landslide. Tom could find no other word to describe it.

The rocky path they'd been following became a living stream, raining down rocks and boulders. The four of them ducked their heads and huddled protectively in a tight circle, their arms locked around each other.

The noise was deafening, as though the earth itself was shattering into pieces. The force of the landslide enveloped them all in a choking cloud of dust and debris. Enormous rocks careened wildly around them, slamming against the scavengers. The boulders flattened the creatures and pitched them down the slope.

Then, as suddenly as it had begun, it was over.

The massive landslide ended, leaving nothing but a trickle of pebbles sliding down the path. As the earth settled Tom raised his head, wiped the dirt from his eyes, and looked around.

He shifted his gaze to his friends, where he saw the same amazement he felt reflected on their dust-coated faces. They unlocked their arms and stepped away from each other, each of them carefully scanning their surroundings.

The scavengers were gone. Not a single stinking, slimy creature remained.

A slow, beaming smile broke across Willa's face. She looked at Tom. "It worked," she said. "The folly's wish. It actually worked."

Porter tossed back his head and gave a whoop of joy. "You did it!" he said, looking at Tom. He threw his arms open wide. "I warned you not to use it, but you did, and look, nothing went wrong—"

His words were cut off by a sharp cracking sound. The ground where he stood, weakened by the slide, abruptly split apart.

The earth opened up and swallowed Porter.

It happened that fast.

One second he was there, the next he wasn't. Before Tom could shout a warning, or move, or even blink, his brother was gone.

CHAPTER EIGHTEEN

HERO TWINS

Tom stared at the space where his brother had been. Horror froze him in place. The only part of his body which seemed capable of movement was his heart, which slammed against his ribs, then began beating at triple its normal tempo.

Umbrey's words raced through his mind. *Your wish will be granted, but always at a cost.*

Porter's. *One of these times your luck's going to run out. You're going to try to play hero and end up killing somebody. I don't want to be around when that happens.*

Too late. Tom's stomach clenched. They'd both warned him, but he hadn't listened.

"*No!*" Willa's agonized scream ripped through the air. She raced to the spot where Porter had last stood and fell to her knees, peering into the gaping chasm. "*Porter!*"

Tom rushed to her side, kneeled down, and screamed for his brother. "*Porter!*"

A second later Mudge was beside them. "*Porter!*"

Nothing. No sound. No echo. No reply.

Porter was gone. Just . . . gone.

Tom peered inside the rocky slit in the earth, but couldn't make out anything. All he could see were craggy walls and darkness without end, possibly stretching all the way to the center of the earth.

He threw one leg over and moved to drop inside.

Willa grabbed his arm to stop him. "Wait!" she cried, clearly terrified. "What are you doing?"

"Going in to find him."

"But—it could be full of scavengers. Or worse. You don't know what's down there."

"Yeah, I do," he answered. "Porter's down there. And I'm going to find him."

Willa blinked. "Of course. We'll go with you."

"No. I'll do it."

She looked ready to argue, so Tom pressed his point. "If Porter's down there, he's probably hurt. I'll need your help getting him back up. We've got to work together. The faster we do this, the better." He scanned the surrounding area and pointed to a heavy boulder. "While I'm gone, take your ropes and tie them to that rock. See if you can make some sort of sling—something we can use to pull him back up."

"He's right," Mudge said. "Let's get the sling ready, then wait until we know what else we can do to help."

Tom was once again struck by the maturity in Mudge's voice, by his cool certainty.

He swung his other leg over. "I'll come right back. I promise." He hesitated for a moment, then continued, "But in case something happens—"

"It won't," Willa said firmly.

"*In case*," Tom said. "If I'm not back in ten minutes, take Mudge and get off this island. Don't wait. Get back to the *Crimson Belle* as fast as you can."

"I understand." A small, quivering smile curved her lips. "But we won't have to. You'll find Porter and he'll be okay. We'll get the sling ready, just in case." She gave a firm nod, as though reassuring herself as much as Tom. "It's getting late. Hurry."

"I will."

Tom lowered himself into the narrow crevice. He pushed

away all thoughts of what might be waiting for him below and focused on the climb. Straight down, one hand over the other, moving from foothold to foothold, his body tightly pressed against the stone face.

To his surprise, the climb was astonishingly easy. He'd scaled more difficult walls at the Lost Academy. Granted, the opening crevice was narrow and dark, but once he scooted past the initial twelve foot drop, he found himself on a spiral staircase made of stone. He raced down the twisting stairs, moving deeper and deeper into the earth, until he came to a vast, cave-like room carved from the same pinkish stone he'd seen everywhere in Arx.

He nearly tripped over the figure lying at the base of the stairs.

Porter.

His brother was sprawled out on his back. As Tom knelt beside him, Porter rose to a half-sitting position and propped himself up on his elbows. Tom performed a quick mental inventory of his injuries. He was scraped and bruised, but he didn't look like he was seriously injured. He simply looked . . . annoyed.

"What took you so long?" Porter snapped.

Tom's relief was so intense his knees almost buckled. "I thought I killed you."

"Not yet. But I have no doubt you'll keep trying."

"You all right?"

"Absolutely. Everyone should be swallowed by the earth and pitched down a stone staircase. I highly recommend it."

Obviously his penchant for sarcasm hadn't been impaired by his fall. "Can you stand?" Tom asked.

Porter shook his head and pointed to a fallen boulder pinning his ankle. "My leg's trapped."

With as much force as Tom could muster, he pushed his

shoulder against the rock. It wouldn't budge. He twisted around and peered closer. "Look, I think it's just the cloth that's caught. If you take off your boots and slip off your pants, you should be able to get your leg free."

Porter glared at him. "I'm not going to face the crews of the *Purgatory* and the *Crimson Belle* dressed in my underwear. Give it another shove."

"You're being an idiot."

"Am I? Fine. Then give me *your* pants."

Tom planted his feet against the stone wall, leaned his shoulder against the boulder and shoved.

"Yeah, that's what I thought." Porter planted his free foot against the stone, the muscles in his thigh quivering as he shoved against it. "This is my home," he panted. "I don't want to be a laughingstock the rest of my life. You can leave, go back to your world. But this is all I have."

"Shut up. You've said that before, but it's not true and you know it."

"Oh, really?"

"Really," Tom dug in, straining against the rock. "You've got me."

Porter released a sharp bark of laughter. "Obviously I must not already be in enough pain for you."

The boulder rocked a tiny bit, and together they gave a final, backbreaking shove. The stone wobbled, and then rolled free. Porter let out a long, low groan. He lifted his ankle, wincing as he flexed it experimentally.

Tom, his muscles nearly liquefied from the effort of moving the boulder, sank to the stone floor. Breathing hard, he sat with his knees drawn up, his back pressed against the wall. He turned his head slightly and looked at Porter. "You might act like a complete jerk at times, but you're still my brother."

For a long moment, Porter didn't speak. Then he let out a deep breath and raked his fingers through his hair. "The Hero Twins," he muttered. "Do you hate that name as much as I do?"

Caught completely off-guard, Tom blinked in surprise.

"Actually, yeah, I do."

"Because it sounds like we're nothing unless we're together?"

Well, more because Tom was absolutely certain he wasn't hero material, and also because the name sounded like a couple of idiots who ran around in spandex and capes. But as his brother seemed to have more on his mind, he simply nodded and let him continue.

"For a while," Porter said, "after you left, it was fine. Mudge had taken the throne, we had a new council in place, and everything was under control."

Tom arched a dark brow and looked at him. "Under control?"

"Well, almost."

"Right." Tom lifted his hand, ticking off fingers as he spoke. "Divino virtually abandoned, Keegan raving mad and chained in a dungeon, the Sword of Five Kingdoms effectively powerless, and dozens of undead roaming the streets." He shook his head. "It might not have been as tight and organized as you thought."

A ghost of a smile flitted across Porter's lips. "So maybe a few things needed a minor adjustment."

"Yeah, maybe." He shrugged. "It must have been bad, or Mudge and Willa wouldn't have sent Umbrey to find me."

"What?"

"Mudge and Willa sent Umbrey to find me."

"No. I sent Umbrey to find you. I knew we needed you."

Their eyes locked, and Tom felt a tug between them—an emotional pull that was part debt, part obligation, and part something else. Whatever it was, it was the first time they'd connected without a map between them.

"The Hero Twins," Porter said, shaking his head in disgust. "I guess we're stuck with it."

"I guess so." Although actually, now that he thought about

it, maybe the name wasn't so bad after all. Tom stood, watching as Porter rose and gingerly took a step. "How's your ankle?"

"It hurts."

"You'll get over it."

Porter glared at him. "Do you have any idea how completely aggravating you are?"

"Because I used the folly's rattle even though you warned me not to?"

"No. Because your idiotic stunts always seem to work out, and mine never do."

"I almost got you killed." Tom held up the folly's rattle. "This didn't exactly work out."

"Yeah, it did."

Porter pointed upward. Until that moment, it hadn't occurred to Tom to wonder where the light was coming from, or how he was able to see if they were in an underground room. He tipped back his head and saw pale shafts of light filtering in through the arched recesses of a tall, cylindrical building. His jaw dropped open. He snapped it shut and looked at Porter.

Porter nodded. "An underground entrance. We're inside the tower."

"I'll get Willa and Mudge."

Tom turned and took off.

CHAPTER NINETEEN

DARK LEAP

Together the four of them raced up the spiral stairs leading to the top of the tower, Porter limping, but keeping pace. At last they reached the very top where they could see thick smoke billowing from a volcano. Tom peered through a crumpled opening of the tower. He knew from the map that the Island of Despair and the Island of Death were also near. He was glad they did not have to venture that way.

Tom turned, expecting to find a room. Instead they were on a circular, open-air platform of sorts. Tall arched columns carved from dark, highly polished granite wrapped around them on all sides, through which a vicious wind howled.

It was almost dark. As the sun set, the gathering twilight cast an eerie greenish-gray glow over everything. But there still remained enough light for them to see—especially as their attention was focused on just one thing.

155

In the center of the floor was a single stone column, approximately waist high. The Black Book of Pernicus floated above it. Despite sharp gusts of wind tearing through the space, the book hovered completely undisturbed, not so much as a page fluttering.

They edged cautiously toward it. Willa reached for it first, and was promptly rewarded with an electric shock that sent her flying backwards. As she hit the ground, the stone floor shook as though rattled by an earthquake. Tom helped her to her feet and they moved toward it once again.

Porter reached for it next. He stretched a single finger toward the book and received a sharp, biting shock. The tower trembled again, the entire structure flexing and heaving as though it were on the verge of collapse. Porter swore and took a deep breath to brace himself, then drew back his arm as though ready to plunge it through the electrical force field and grab the book.

"*Don't!*"

Tom grabbed his arm, stopping him.

Porter jerked free. "What are you doing?"

"The tower's rigged," Tom said. "You grab the book, and this whole place will fall down on top of us."

As he spoke, the tower swayed like a skyscraper in an earthquake, the floor trembling in silent protest to their very presence.

"Wait a minute," Porter blurt out. "Let me see if I understand you. The book is *right there*. Right in front of us. But if we grab it, we'll be buried under twenty tons of rock."

Tom nodded. "I think so."

"So you're saying we should just give up? *Now?*"

Tom looked at his brother. "No. I'm saying we don't touch the book until we can get out of here fast. Real fast. Before this tower collapses on top of us."

"And how do you suggest we do that?"

"Fly."

Tom removed the coiled rope he'd been carrying and flung it down—they wouldn't need it anymore. Then he opened Willa's satchel and removed the four brass cleats he'd taken from Zaputo's ship. Setting them aside, he moved to one of the granite archways at the edge of the tower. Far beneath him, fierce waves crashed against jagged rocks at the base of the cliff. The Cursed Souls Sea frothed and foamed, churning violently.

Willa came to stand beside him. She peered across the water. "Look! I think I see the *Crimson Belle*. It's waiting for us!"

"Perfect." Tom took off the coarse red outer shirt Umbrey's crewman had given him and began waving it in the direction of the ship.

"What are you doing?" asked Porter.

"Signaling." Tom looked at his brother. "Remember what you said? The best way to get from the tower back to the *Crimson Belle* was if we could fly? We can't. But Zaputo's bird can. That's the answer. You said it. I just put the pieces together."

Porter shook his head. "I wish I knew what you're talking about."

Tom caught a glimpse of a distant spec in the twilight, a spec that grew larger and larger as it fluttered toward them. "You'll see."

The crimson bird darted between the columns. It circled over their heads, hissing and cawing, then released a single, glistening gold object from its talons. Tom caught it in his palm as the bird darted away.

"Saved by the bell," he murmured.

He held it up for Porter and Willa to see. They moved closer to examine it, their faces clouded with confusion. Porter scowled and shook his head. "A jingle bell? The bell from Zaputo's slipper? That's your plan? That's how we're going to get back to the *Crimson Belle*?"

"No," Tom corrected him. "Not just a jingle bell. A jingle bell with a silk thread attached to it."

He began pulling the thread as fast as he could, drawing

it toward him until it began to feel heavy. A run of fine netting was knotted to the end of the thread. He pulled yard after yard of the netting until he reached a length of slim rope. He dragged that in, hand over hand, until he reached the coarse, heavy rope that would hold their weight and carry them back to the Crimson Belle.

"Brilliant," Willa breathed.

Tom looked at Porter. "Can you tie a knot that won't slip loose?"

At Porter's nod, he handed him the end of the rope. Porter secured it to a pair of heavy stone columns. "Now what? We climb down the rope to the ship? It's too far. Even if the tower doesn't collapse on us, our arms will give out before we get halfway there."

Tom shook his head and lifted a slick brass cleat. It was slightly curved, highly polished and smooth, with a bulky knob at either end for gripping. He positioned it across the top of the rope line.

"Where I come from," he said, "this is called a zip line."

He explained how the concept worked. One end of the rope was tied to a stone column in the tower. The opposite end was tied to the main mast of the Crimson Belle. All they had to do was position the cleat over the top of the rope, grab the brass ends, and jump. Gravity would glide them down to the ship's deck.

Tom looked at Porter. "It's not flying, but it's pretty close. It might just work."

"Might?"

"Will."

"Listen," Willa said, going suddenly still.

Tom knew from the look on her face what he'd hear. He cocked his head and listened anyway. The low moan of scavengers echoed up from the spiral staircase. They'd found the underground entrance. He shot a glance around the room. The staircase simply opened up to the top floor. There was no door, nothing they could use to barricade themselves in—or keep the scavengers out.

A lantern flashed in the distance, Zaputo's signal that the rope was secured on his end.

Porter looked at Tom. "I don't suppose you could think of another way to get us back to the ship?"

"Afraid not."

"Is it safe?"

Technically, it was. Especially if they had adequate ropes, cables, helmets, safety harnesses, elbow and knee pads, and a thick foam landing spot. But as they didn't have any of that, Tom modified his answer slightly. "As long as you don't let go."

"Perfect. I think I figured out that much already." Porter's mouth tightened as the sound of the scavengers grew louder. Except this time the sound was coming from a different direction.

Tom leaned forward, peering over the edge of the floor. Dozens of scavengers scaled the coarse outer walls of the tower, clawing their way upward. Now the creatures were coming toward them from both *inside* and *outside* the tower. The entire tower was erupting in scavengers. They were trapped. No way to escape except the zip line—if it worked.

"Get ready," he said. "I'll grab the book and—"

"No. We'll use my sword," Mudge said, lifting the Sword of Five Kingdoms.

Like sticking a knife in an electric circuit, Tom thought. He pushed the blade away. "Try it and it'll kill you."

"No it won't," Willa said firmly. "He's right."

Porter shook his head. "What are you talking about?"

"Whatever's protecting that book doesn't know us, but it will recognize the sword," she said. "I should have thought of that sooner. Half of the blade belonged to Pernicus, remember?"

"Just do it fast," Tom urged.

Holding the sword aloft, Mudge

stepped forward and touched the tip of the blade to the space in front of the book. An orbit of neon sparks showered the book, revealing a glowing green mist swirling around it.

He gently waved the blade back and forth, as though brushing the sparks aside. A dark hole appeared in the swirling field of green mist. Mudge thrust his fist through the hole. He grabbed the book and jerked it out. The neon sparks went black, abruptly extinguishing themselves.

Done. Tom looked at the slim black volume Mudge held. He looked at Porter, then at Willa. At Mudge. For a moment, none of them moved. Then slow, beaming smiles broke out across their faces.

"We got it," Willa said.

"We did," Porter agreed.

A sharp gust of wind whipped around them. The floor buckled and shook. The tower shuddered. It heaved. One granite column collapsed, then another, and another, crashing to the floor like dominoes.

"*Go!*" Tom shouted. "*Now!*"

Mudge passed the book to Tom, who tucked it into Willa's satchel slung across his chest. Mudge moved to the edge of the tower, positioned his brass cleat over the rope, gripped the ends, and jumped.

Moving at an alarming rate, he shot down the rope and disappeared into the darkening twilight.

Tom peered into the darkness after him. He couldn't see anything. There was no way to tell if he had made it to the ship, or been swallowed by the sea.

Willa was next. Her face pale, she stepped to the edge of the tower floor and readied her cleat. The wind whipped around her, so intense it was a struggle for her just to stand.

"Don't look down," Tom advised, raising his voice over the

roar of the wind. "Just hold on tight and jump. The line will carry you straight to the ship."

The scavenger's moans grew louder. Their putrid odor drifted up the stairs. They'd almost reached the top. Willa muttered a brief prayer, closed her eyes, and leapt. She shot down the rope, disappearing as quickly as Mudge had.

The tower pitched and swayed. The western edge of the structure crumbled, raining rocks and debris down on the ground below.

Tom thrust a cleat at Porter. "Go. I'll be right behind you."

"But—"

"*Go.*"

Porter looked as though he wanted to argue, but seemed to think better of it. He positioned his cleat and jumped.

The first scavenger stumbled up the staircase and staggered to the surface.

Tom sized the creature up. Enormous, male, with what appeared to be a large part of its brain oozing down its scalp. It sniffed the air like a beast locating its prey, then swung around and lunged toward him.

The scavenger hissed in excitement as his long yellowed fingernails caught Tom's shirt.

The tower gave a final shudder. The floor split in two and gave way.

Tom wasn't going to make it. Not now. Not with the tower crumbling into pieces, cracking and heaving and hurling itself toward the ground. Not with the scavenger tearing at his clothes.

But he had to try.

He positioned his cleat, grabbed the brass ends, and jumped.

CHAPTER TWENTY

BLACK BOOK

A vertical freefall. Tom was headed straight for the jagged rocks below. Or at least it felt that way. Then the rope seemed to catch, tensing a bit beneath his weight. He felt a slight bounce as the line straightened out, sending him shooting over the Cursed Souls Sea and carrying him directly toward the *Crimson Belle*.

The air exploded with a thundering rumble and the tower collapsed behind him. The rope on which he was gliding abruptly dipped. Tom could feel the slackening of tension on the line itself. He was dropping fast. But he was nearly there . . . so close . . .

The ship's main mast suddenly loomed in front of him, and Tom realized there was no way for him to slow down for landing. There was no way for him to stop at all. He was about to slam face first into a thick wooden mast. He braced himself for impact, knowing there was a very strong likelihood he was about to end up looking a lot like the scavenger he just left up in the tower.

No sooner had he resigned himself to that fate when he felt a bone-jarring thud. Two of Zaputo's crewmen tackled him as though he were a football dummy, knocking him off the zip line and sending him flying into a thick stack of canvas sails.

He lay motionless for a second, then slowly eased himself up into a sitting position. He put a hand to his head. His skull was still intact, though he had to shake his head to clear his vision. The first thing that swam into view was Willa. Then Porter and Mudge. They swayed on their feet, looking exactly how he felt—absolutely stunned to still be alive.

Before Tom could say a word to them, or even *think* of what he might say, Zaputo stepped before him, wearing silk pantaloons and a brightly colored vest. He stood with his feet planted firmly on the deck, his bulging biceps crossed over his broad chest, his thick gold necklace glittering in the lantern's light. The crimson bird once again rode on his shoulder.

"You have the Black Book of Pernicus?" Zaputo demanded.

Tom nodded.

"Give it here."

He hesitated. It had almost cost them their lives to get it, so naturally he was reluctant to simply hand it over. On the other hand, even if he resisted, 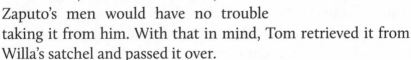 Zaputo's men would have no trouble taking it from him. With that in mind, Tom retrieved it from Willa's satchel and passed it over.

Zaputo studied the book for a moment, weighing it in his hands. Then he looked at Tom. "This will rid our lands of the scavengers?"

"That's what I've been told."

Zaputo attempted to open the book, but no matter how much he tugged at the pages, he couldn't pry it open.

Tom shook his head. "Keegan and Mudge must open it together. It won't work for anyone else."

Zaputo transferred his gaze to Mudge. "Is this true?" he demanded.

Anyone else might have trembled under the weight of Zaputo's dark stare. Mudge merely nodded. "Yes."

"Then I will keep it safe until we arrive."

"Very good," Mudge said. "You may." With that, he gave a regal nod of dismissal.

Zaputo stood motionless for a long moment, scowling down at Mudge. Watching him, Tom couldn't help but wonder if Zaputo saw the same chameleon-like quality in Mudge that he had noticed. And if so, he wondered what his thoughts were about Mudge's uncanny ability to slip so effortlessly between young boy and dignified ruler.

But whatever they were, Zaputo kept them to himself. Turning to his crew, he bellowed, "Divino!" and strode toward the quarterdeck.

Willa and Porter watched him walk away. Then they sank down beside Tom on the pile of sailcloth. Mudge collapsed next to them. Exhausted, Tom leaned back and stared up at the sky, gazing at the early evening stars. Actually, exhausted wasn't even a strong enough word for what he felt. He was so tired his bones ached.

Zaputo's crew adjusted the sails and the *Crimson Belle* veered about, heading back out into the agitated waters of the Cursed Souls Sea. One of the former captives brought them water, another brought food, and still another brought blankets. Their gestures were kind, but they did nothing to shake the bleak sense of worry that settled over Tom.

The Black Book of Pernicus.

They'd finally retrieved it, so he should have relaxed. Instead, the opposite was true. Tension churned through him, setting his nerves on edge. The book was evil. He'd felt that in the brief moments he'd held it in his hands. That was the problem. They had to open it if they wanted to find a way to rid the kingdom of scavengers. But opening it would only subject them to more evil.

His thoughts spun around and around in fruitless circles, just as they'd physically circled the tower at Arx. The key, the sword, the book. There must be a solution, but it remained outside his mental grasp. Their efforts to gain the book had taken a toll. His brain was simply too foggy for him to think properly, and the rough seas through which they traveled didn't help him focus.

His gaze fell on Mudge, who'd fallen sound asleep the moment he'd finished eating. Tom shook his head, amazed at the boy's ability to sleep when so much was still at stake.

Finally they reached the Coral Canyon. It had been nearly impossible to cross in the bright light of day. Tom had no idea how Zaputo hoped to repeat the feat in the dead of night. Surely they would be ripped to shreds. As it turned out, however, he needn't have worried.

Umbrey waited for them on the other side of the canyon, the *Purgatory* lit up like a Christmas tree. Brightly blazing lanterns hung from the masts, the beams, the crow's nest, the stern, the port, the ship's rail. Every inch of the vessel was aglow. The ship burned brighter than a lighthouse. A shining beacon meant to lead them safely through the Coral Canyon and back to Divino.

That was the last thing Tom saw before the exhaustion he'd been battling got the best of him. Sleep dragged him under. But it wasn't a restful sleep. In his dreams, the image of the Zaputo's hungry bird flashed before his eyes. Only this time *he* was the one being pecked apart, not some flopping fish. As he fought to escape, the howling laughter of Pernicus echoed in his ears.

Ten minutes before midnight, the *Crimson Belle* and the *Purgatory* sailed through the walled gates of Divino—the very gates Tom had leapt from only days ago, though it seemed much longer ago than that—and docked in the warehouse district. As they disembarked, Keegan's army was there to greet them. The Watch lined the streets, dressed in their signature black capes with the glowing red eye fixed at the shoulder clasp.

Three of Keegan's men stepped before Umbrey and Zaputo.

"You will come with us," said the largest of the group, raising his sword and holding it before his chest.

Umbrey arched a single brow. He glanced over his shoulder. "Such a pretty invitation, lads. What do you think, should we accept?"

"Yes," replied Zaputo, his face stony.

"Yes," said Mudge.

"Well, there you have it!" Umbrey brought his hands together in a sharp clap and rubbed them briskly. "Excellent, gentlemen. We're all in agreement. Lead on. It's time to finish this thing."

They walked though the streets in pairs. Umbrey and Zaputo (with Zaputo's crimson bird riding on his shoulder), Willa and Mudge, Tom and Porter. A few of Umbrey's crew, along with a few of Zaputo's men, trailed behind them.

Tom noted that while they had been away, Keegan had managed to barricade the city. A blazing ring of fire surrounded them, pushing the scavengers out of the inner district. Though he couldn't see the creatures, there was no doubt they were there. Their distinct moans echoed through the streets and their rancid scent hung in the air.

Keegan's men led them to the courthouse, opened the door, and ushered them inside. Keegan waited for them on the elevated stage that had once been the judge's box. But that juror's compartment had been removed. In its place he had installed his throne.

"My, my, my," he purred as they entered, leaning back in his velvet seat. "You do like a dramatic entrance, don't you?" He cocked his head and put a hand to his ear, listening as the clock in the market tower struck midnight. "Right as the bell tolls. How *very* stirring."

His gaze slowly traveled over Tom, Porter, Willa, and Mudge.

"I trust you had an enjoyable journey," he said. "How wonderful it is for young people to have the opportunity to travel. Broaden their horizons and all that. And a cruise, no less. Exciting."

Umbrey sighed. "God, man. You do like to prattle on, don't you?"

Moving with panther-like grace, Keegan slid from his throne and slowly circled Umbrey. "Umbrey. Delighted to see you back in one piece." He paused, staring pointedly at Umbrey's peg leg. "Oh. Forgive me. I meant to say, *almost* one piece."

"You are wasting my time," Zaputo announced.

Keegan turned. "Ah, Zaputo. My burly friend. Welcome. What brings you to our little party?"

"The Black Book of Pernicus."

Keegan's gaze sharpened. "You have it?"

Zaputo reached inside his vest and removed the slim black volume. He held it up. Keegan reached for it, but Zaputo drew back before he could touch it.

"My ship and crew were used to retrieve this book. Therefore you will hear my terms before you have it."

Tom cut a questioning glance at Porter and Willa. Their expressions mirrored the same confusion and apprehension he felt. Mudge, however, merely looked curious—or rather, intently interested in hearing Zaputo's terms.

A slow smile broke across Keegan's face. "Ah. Well done. Exactly what I would do in your position, Zaputo. Let that be a lesson, children. Power is only effective if you aren't afraid to use it."

"Open this book," Zaputo said, "and there will be no further contact between the people of Aquat and the people of Divino. Ever. We will not come to your land, you will not come to ours."

The statement hung in the air between them. "Dictating terms, are we?" asked Keegan.

"Yes."

"Very well." Keegan gave a cool nod and rapped his nails together. "Here are *my* terms: I will take the book, and use the people of Aquat in any way that pleases me."

"No," countered a low, female voice, "*I* will take the book." Zaputo's fiery bird dove from its perch on his shoulder and snatched the book away. The bird soared over their heads, then allowed the volume to slip through its talons, dropping it into the hands of a dark-haired woman who had stepped quietly into the room.

Vivienne.

Beautiful, deadly, cold, and calculating. The woman who'd guarded the Lost Lake and the Sword of Five Kingdoms—and had threatened to drown them all if they failed to retrieve it.

Beside him, Umbrey drew in a sharp, horrified gasp, as Tom finally put the pieces together. The crimson bird. He *knew* it was familiar. But the last time he'd seen the creature it had been part of a pair. One gleaming white bird and one deep ruby. Both of which had led them to Vivienne.

Once again, the bird had acted on behalf of its master, drawing them toward the ruthless Vivienne.

"Excellent," she breathed. "The Black Book of Pernicus. I hold it at last." She ran her hands over the worn leather cover. "Marrick is gone. Pernicus is gone. Yet I remain. And now the book is mine. All good things come to those who wait."

Umbrey pivoted furiously glaring at Keegan. "Do you have any idea what you've done?"

"I've made an alliance," Keegan replied curtly. "An alliance that will bring the Five Kingdoms back under my control. Permanently."

"No," Umbrey countered. "You have given the book to the one person who will take that power and use it to destroy us all."

"How you flatter me." Vivienne's lips curved upward in a smile of icy contempt. She turned toward the window and looked outside. A second later, the din of crashing wood echoed through the street, followed by the shouts and screams of voices raised in panic. Vivienne looked at the group and gave an elegant shrug.

"A shame," she said. "Your precious barricades must have fallen." She set the Black Book of Pernicus atop a table and backed away, looking expectantly at Keegan. "The key."

The darkness that had marked Keegan's expression only seconds earlier turned to naked greed, tinged with excitement so great his fingers shook. He removed his key and pressed it against the rough leather cover. The volume trembled, then the pages fluttered open.

Vivienne released a long, deep breath. She reverently traced her fingers over the pages, then swung around to look at Mudge. "Well, Marrick's chosen?" she demanded. "What are you waiting for? Do you want to rid your lands of scavengers? The power of Pernicus is here, within these pages."

"Yes," Mudge said. "It is."

"Then bring it to life. Release it with that sword of yours."

"No!" shouted Umbrey. "Don't do it, lad!"

"*Silence!*" hissed Vivienne.

The howls and moans of the scavengers drew closer.

Tom's breath caught in his throat. Mudge moved toward the book. He glanced around the room and gave a decisive nod. Then, in a movement so fast it was little more than a blur, he lifted his sword and drove it through the spine of the book.

"*No!*" Vivienne cried, reaching for the volume. She was too late.

The Black Book of Pernicus lit up, shooting out rays of brilliant green light. Then it emitted a long, slow hiss and the pages blackened, curling in on themselves as though touched by fire. Within seconds, all that remained was a pile of smoldering ash.

"*No!*" roared Keegan, lunging toward Mudge.

Zaputo caught him and shoved him toward his crewmen.

"Take him below and chain him up," ordered Mudge. "The same with his men."

Keegan looked at Vivienne. "Kill them!" he roared, his face red with rage. "Kill them all! Every one of them."

Vivienne returned his look with one of complete indifference. "You have failed me," she said, watching as Keegan and his men were dragged to the basement cell.

Tom heard Keegan's protests, his shrill threats, then the satisfying clamor of the iron bars rattling shut. Keegan was captive once again.

The crimson bird perched itself on the windowsill. Vivienne moved to stand just beneath the window. She surveyed them all with an expression of icy calm. "The mapmaker's sons," she said. "Enjoy your victory here, for it will not last long. Even as we speak, the passage to Terrum has been opened. You're too late to stop me."

The bird beat its wings and dove into the room, flying straight toward them. Tom ducked, as did everyone else. When he straightened again—only to watch the bird shoot out of the window—Vivienne was gone.

"What did she mean, 'the passage is open'?" Tom asked.

"The Bloody Passage," Porter answered grimly. "The passage that protects the people of Terrum from northern invaders."

"Why? What does she want?" Willa asked.

"The power that Marrick and Pernicus denied her."

"But—"

"Never mind that now," Umbrey said. "One battle at a time, lads." He opened the courtroom door and stepped outside. A moment later he reentered the room, a beaming smile on his scruffy face. "That's the most beautiful silence I've ever heard."

Silence? Tom darted outside, followed by Willa and

Porter. Nothing. No moans, no groans, no unearthly growls. No scavengers. Already the stench of the creatures was beginning to lift.

They raced back inside. "How did you know?" Willa asked, looking at Mudge. "How did you know destroying the book would destroy the scavengers?"

Mudge looked at her, surprised. "Tom and Porter showed me."

Tom and Porter exchanged astonished glances. "*We* showed you? When?"

"Keegan asked you both to use the map to show him the book. You did. When he placed his key on it, the pages opened. That was the only power Keegan had. But the sword . . . " Mudge thought for a moment, absently tapping the blade among the ashes of the book. "Good *or* evil. A choice. A balance between the two. I held the *choice* of whether to release what was in the book, or end it once and for all."

"What about The Watch?" said Tom.

To Tom's surprise, it wasn't Mudge who answered, but Zaputo. "If you cut the head from a scorpion, the tail will eventually die as well."

"Exactly," Mudge said, nodding approvingly at Zaputo. "Keegan's trial will resume. Those who came to his defense, including The Watch, will be captured and punished. And as to Vivienne, we'll find her . . . or she'll find us."

"So it's over then?" Tom said.

Mudge shook his head. "Not quite." Turning, he mounted the stairs and seated himself on Keegan's throne. His gaze locked on Zaputo. "You had terms for Keegan. You wanted no contact between the people of Aquat and the people of Divino. Keegan would not accept those terms. Neither will I."

A heavy silence filled the room.

Zaputo raised his chin. "The people of Aquat will no longer be used to ferry slaves from Divino."

"There will be no more slaves from Divino," Mudge replied. "Those days are past. I give you my word."

"The people of Aquat will need to find another way to earn money to buy food."

"The people of Divino will need money as well. Money to rebuild the damage the scavengers have done."

Silence fell. They seemed to have reached an impasse. Mudge lifted his sword. Its brilliance had returned. He twisted it from side to side, watching as the blade glistened with an ethereal white light. "Keegan said something before I left to search for the book. He said I expected to just wave my magic sword and watch all the problems of the Five Kingdoms disappear. He was right—the sword doesn't work that way." He looked at Zaputo, his gaze intent. "Do you know why?"

Zaputo was silent for a long moment. He regarded Mudge with a look that was part curiosity, part suspicion, as though he feared he was being led into a trap. After a long pause he said, "Why?"

"The power of this sword was never in the blade. But here, in the hilt." He ran his fingers over the five shiny black stones embedded in the sword's grip. "Five kingdoms, united to work together, prosper together, and protect each other."

His words sent a chill down Tom's spine. He heard Porter's sharp intake of breath, and watched as a small, proud smile curved Willa's lips.

Zaputo remained unimpressed. "What are you asking?"

"The island of Arx. A city as old as time. It was once a busy port, a center for all the kingdoms to come together and trade their goods. It is time to rebuild Arx, to restore it to its former glory. If the people of Aquat and Divino work together, we can accomplish that."

Excitement lit Zaputo's dark eyes as he considered the prospect. When he spoke, however, his words were cautious.

"That would be an expensive undertaking."

"True." Mudge nodded solemnly. Then he turned to Tom, Porter, and Willa. "Do you remember when Porter fell into the underground chamber?"

Tom nodded. He'd never forget it.

"I had some time to look around as I waited for you to return. As you remember, the landslide disturbed quite a bit of ground. Part of what churned to the surface was this."

Mudge held out his hand.

Gold. A glistening nugget the size of a raisin rested in his palm.

Mudge's narrow chest swelled with pride. An expression of boyish glee flitted over his face. "Salamaine never found it, but we did."

Umbrey gave a *whoop* of delight. Willa wrapped her arms around Tom and Porter and squeezed them both. "Yes!"

"To an alliance between our countries," Mudge said. He stood and raised his sword, tilting it toward Zaputo. "From this day forward, we work together, prosper together, protect each other."

Zaputo studied Mudge in silence. He removed his own sword, an enormous glittering cutlass, from his belt. "You have my allegiance." He tapped his blade against Mudge's.

The moment the blades touched, the Sword of Five Kingdoms began to glow. Its blinding white energy shot down Zaputo's cutlass. Then a sharp metallic rattling sound echoed across the room. For a moment, Tom assumed it was simply the blades touching, but the sound continued even after the two swords pulled apart.

It took them all a moment to recognize the source of the noise. Zaputo's necklace. The ornate golden orb suspended from his chain trembled and shook.

Frowning, Zaputo lifted the orb and touched the trigger, allowing it to snap open. The mana seed fell into his palm. But it was no longer dry and hard. As they watched, the seed grew plump and round. A delicate green shoot sprouted from the center.

Zaputo's mouth dropped open. He staggered backward, too overwhelmed to speak.

Umbrey smiled and turned toward Mudge. "Looks like the power in your blade has returned, majesty."

The room erupted in joyful chaos. Tom, Willa, and Porter swarmed Mudge. Zaputo's crewmen rushed to study the mana seed, touching it in awe. Even Umbrey's crew, rough as they were, seemed happily shaken by the turn of events.

As the noise finally died down, Willa caught Tom's hand and gave it a squeeze. "You'll stay this time, right?"

Tom's gaze moved from Willa, to Porter, to Mudge. Yes. He wanted to stay. He wanted to be a part of whatever happened next. At least until they knew what was happening in Terrum.

But before he could reply, Umbrey answered for him. "I'm afraid he can't. Not this time." He looked at Tom. "Professor Lost was very adamant about that. No dilly-dallying. He said something about his list?"

The demerits. Tom's heart sank.

Umbrey gave his shoulder a sympathetic pat. "You're going home, lad. We leave with the tide tomorrow morning."

CHAPTER TWENTY-ONE

MORTIMER LOST

Morning came early. As they'd all been too exhausted to look for other arrangements, they'd borrowed blankets and linens normally used for the prisoners and made beds for themselves on the stone floor. Umbrey had warned Tom that they would leave right after first light, but as it had been well past midnight when they'd finally all gone to sleep, Tom had been skeptical of their early departure. He shouldn't have been. As soon as a soft pink glow touched the horizon, he was awakened by the steady thump of Umbrey's peg leg striding across the floor.

"Rise and shine, lad! It's a glorious day for a sail." He deposited a stack of clothing—Tom's Lost Academy uniform, now clean and pressed and ready to wear—at the foot of his bed.

Tom groaned, but resisted the urge to dive back under the covers. By the time he dressed and made his way downstairs, he found Willa, Porter, and Mudge waiting for him.

Willa stepped forward immediately and wrapped Tom in a tight hug. Tom hesitantly returned her embrace, feeling more than a little awkward. He wasn't used to being squeezed by girls. Finally she gave a dramatic sigh and drew back. "Saying good-bye is always the worst."

"I'll miss Tom," Mudge said, "but I think being chased by a mob of hungry scavengers is worse."

Willa laughed and shook her head. "Right," she said, then leaned forward and pressed a quick kiss on Tom's cheek. "Come back soon."

Tom froze. He could actually *feel* an idiotic grin forming on his lips, but was completely powerless to remove it. Just as he couldn't stop the fiery blush from heating his cheeks. Needing something, anything else to focus on, he turned away. Tom found himself staring directly into his brother's icy blue eyes.

Tom hesitated, unsure of what to say. *Good-bye? See ya later?* Nothing seemed appropriate.

Porter studied him for a moment in silence, then a wry smile curved his lips. "If you're waiting because you think you're going to get a good-bye kiss from me, don't hold your breath."

Tom laughed. "Best news I've heard all day."

Handshakes followed, and more hugs, and finally it was time to go. Zaputo's men joined them in the courthouse lobby. Apparently they were determined to sail with the first light as well.

As they all moved toward the door, however, Zaputo abruptly stopped. His dark gaze fixed on Tom's tee shirt. He jabbed his thick finger against the Lost Academy insignia embroidered on the pocket. "What is this?" he demanded.

Tom blinked. His gaze shot to Porter, Willa, and Mudge, who looked as confused as he was. "What?"

"Why do you wear this badge?"

"That's . . . " Tom hesitated, not sure what to say. "That's the emblem of the Lost Academy. Mortimer Lost—

"You know Mortimer Lost?"

Tom froze, too stunned to think. Of all the words he would have expected to come from Salvador Zaputo's mouth, *You know Mortimer Lost?* had to be among the most impossible to imagine.

"Yes," Tom finally managed. "I know Mortimer Lost. He's the one who sent me here."

Zaputo's eyes narrowed. "He was your captain before you boarded the *Purgatory*?"

"My . . . my captain?"

Although the words came out as a question, Tom felt the pieces of a puzzle slide firmly into place. The bells. The constant clanging and clamor of bells at mealtimes, bedtime, and classroom shifts. Lost ran the Academy with the same harsh discipline and efficiency as a captain ran a ship. That much he understood. But the rest? Fighting pirates? Exploring dangerous waters? Absolutely not. And yet . . . he'd seen the headmaster, battle lazy instructors, overbearing parents, and classroom bullies, never backing down an inch.

His head spun in confusion. He looked to Umbrey for an answer.

"Aye, lad. You're wearing his insignia. That was Mortimer's flag."

"Mortimer's *flag*?"

"Aye. His flag."

Zaputo let out a breath as a look of relief came over his face. "Twenty-five years ago, I battled your captain. The *Crimson Belle* ran aground and my men and I faced certain death. Mortimer Lost chose to spare our lives." He pressed something into Tom's hand. "Give him this from me. Tell him Salvador Zaputo has paid his debt."

Tom stood near the *Purgatory's* bow, watching the waves strike the hull. Umbrey, apparently satisfied the ship was properly under way, came to join him. Tom looked at him. "I'm worried about Terrum."

"Worrying won't help. If there's something we can do to stop Vivienne, we'll do it. No sense getting worked up about it until we know what we're up against."

Tom sighed, acknowledging the truth of Umbrey's words.

Then he asked, "Why didn't you ever tell me?"

"Tell you what?"

"About Lost."

Umbrey bit into an apple he'd pocketed before leaving the courthouse. He gave a careless shrug, saying around a mouthful of fruit, "I guess I thought you should be able to figure out *some* things for yourself." He glanced over his shoulder at Tom and arched a wiry brow. "You're surprised, lad?"

Surprised? More like astounded. His stiff-backed, narrow-minded, rules-loving, grim-faced, strict disciplinarian headmaster, Mortimer Lost, had once sailed a ship? It was almost impossible to imagine.

"Now *there* was a captain," Umbrey continued, leaning forward to rest his elbows on the ship's rail. A faraway expression came upon him. "Ol' Morty. Completely fearless. He'd sail anywhere, anytime. Tough on his crew, but he never lost a man under his watch, which is a better record than I can boast."

Tom shook his head. "I don't know what to say."

Umbrey smiled. "He's the one who amassed the information your father needed for his maps, you'll remember. His scribe. Gathered stories, interrogated native peoples, surveyed the earth and sky. He taught me everything I know about running a ship

Tom knew Lost and Umbrey had a history, but he never imagined this. He mulled it over. The new knowledge didn't make him *like* Lost. Definitely not. All the same, he felt a small seed of grudging respect take root.

"Never saw a man who loved the sea as much as old Mortimer," Umbrey continued.

"If he loved it so much, why'd he leave it?"

Umbrey looked at him as though the answer should have been perfectly obvious. "Why, to protect you, of course. Keep you out of Keegan's grasp. When your father found a way to the Other Side, there was no other man trusted to bring you there and keep you safe."

Tom's stomach twisted. He felt as though he'd eaten too

178

much of all the wrong things. Lost had given up a life at sea to protect him. Suddenly all his clever pranks didn't seem so clever anymore. Climbing the rooftops, silencing the bells, and most recently, dressing Fred up as a pirate and setting him afloat.

"But why—"

"That's enough, lad. You want to know anything else, you can ask him yourself. We're almost there." Umbrey tilted his chin forward. The mist they'd been sailing through abruptly parted and Tom recognized the Forbidden Lake.

He was home.

Tom had hoped to slip back to his dorm room unnoticed. But the moment he stepped off the Purgatory's gangway and onto the dock, a tall, lanky figure dressed in an old-fashion suit emerged from the shadows near the boathouse.

"Mr. Hawkins," Professor Lost said, "you have returned."

"Yes, sir."

"I trust everything went smoothly?"

Smoothly? Not exactly. Not sure how many details Lost wanted to hear, Tom simply replied, "We destroyed the Black Book of Pernicus. There are no more scavengers."

"Very good. And your voyage? I trust that was satisfactory as well."

"The Purgatory sailed up a waterfall to return here. I would have sworn that was impossible."

Professor Lost sent him a disapproving scowl. "Rarely is anything impossible, Mr. Hawkins. Some things are simply more difficult than others."

As Lost seemed to have a destination in mind, Tom fell into step beside him. They walked in silence until they reached the beach clearing.

"You were a sea captain," Tom said haltingly. "I never knew that."

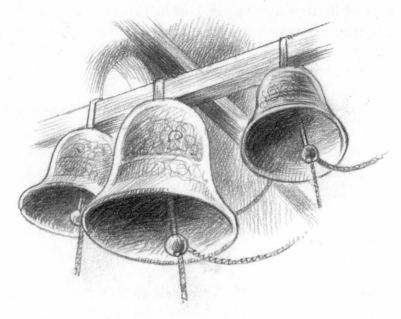

Professor Lost paused, looked at him, then gave a haughty sniff. "I have no doubt the world is full of facts of which you are blissfully ignorant."

"I brought something back for you. From Salvador Zaputo. He says his debt is paid."

He passed Zaputo's necklace to Professor Lost and watched as he opened it.

"Remarkable," Lost muttered. "A mana seed. I never would have dreamed."

"Do you miss the sea?" Tom asked.

Lost gave a beleaguered sigh. "We cannot predict where the tides of life will carry us, Mr. Hawkins. For now, it is my thankless task to try to impart tiny bits of knowledge into your thick skull. I do enjoy a challenge."

"Yes, sir."

"Have you ever been lost, Mr. Hawkins?"

"Lost, sir?"

"It is a simple question. One that is fully within your capabilities to answer." Professor Lost slowly repeated it. "Have you ever been lost?"

Tom thought about it. "No. Never."

"Show me the southeast."

Tom pointed it out immediately.

Lost nodded. "Just as I suspected. An internal compass. A genetic gift given to you by virtue of being the mapmaker's son. I would venture to guess your brother shares the same trait, should you one day care to ask him. Of some use, I suppose. There are several dim-witted fellows among our population here at the academy who would be quite impressed by such gifts."

Tom smiled.

"I, however, am not one of them. Any more than I would be impressed by a man's height or the color of his eyes."

Tom's smile faded.

Lost gave a curt nod. "That which is truly of value rests within each of us. A moral compass. An ability not only to discern right from wrong, but to act upon it—always and without hesitation. Once you truly understand that, then I will have taught you what your father wanted you to know."

"Yes, sir."

"Now then." Lost looked around for a moment, then he selected a shovel left by the groundskeepers and passed it to Tom. He pointed to the ground. "Right there should be fine."

"Sir?"

"A hole, Mr. Hawkins."

Professor Lost watched Tom dig. When he'd finished, he dropped the mana seed inside. Tom covered it up with dirt.

"You think it will bear fruit?" Tom asked.

Professor Lost straightened, locking his hands behind his back. He stared down at Tom. "It's a wonderful and wicked world, Mr. Hawkins. Our actions, our words, our wishes, all have repercussions. Just like the ripples on that lake. We may not know at the time what they are, but we must believe."

"Believe what?"

"One day there will be mana."

Umbrey's voice carried out to them. "Here's the boat you

wanted, Morty!" he said, tugging a wooden rowboat along the edge of the lake.

Lost's brows snapped together. "Do not call me Morty. And that vessel is not for me. It's for Mr. Hawkins."

Tom frowned. "Me, sir?"

"It appears your ill-conceived actions have set off a chain of events, as well. Apparently Fred has been launched again. You will retrieve him at once, then report to my office and we will discuss the appropriate penance for your demerits."

"Yes, sir."

"And while we're there," Umbrey put in, "we might as well take a peek inside that map room of yours, Morty."

"Do not call me—wait. My map room? What business could you possibly have in my map room?"

"Oh, nothing much. Just wondering if there might be another way to Terrum that didn't involve the Bloody Passage. Gets a little messy taking that route, you know."

Lost glared down his nose at Umbrey. "And why would you need to go to Terrum?"

"I'm afraid that's a long story."

"I thought you told me not to worry about it," Tom said.

"Aye, I did. Worrying about it won't help. But preparing for the journey there? Now that's something else." Umbrey gestured toward the boat, then brought his hands together and rubbed them briskly. "But first, the Professor gave you a job to do."

"Yes." Tom climbed in the boat and took a seat.

"Hurry back, lad. We've work to do!"

"Got it." Tom dipped his oars in the water. As he did, his gaze locked on Lost and Umbrey. A look of silent understanding passed between them.

Umbrey smiled. "Just watch you don't row out too far," he called. "That first drop's a doozy."